P9-CQS-624

It's Raining Cupcakes

It's Raining Cupcakes

by LISA SCHROEDER

SCHOLASTIC INC.
New York Toronto London Auckland
Sydney Mexico City New Delhi Hong Kong

This book is a work of fiction. Any references to historical events,
real people, or real locales are used fictitiously. Other names,
characters, places, and incidents are the product of
the author's imagination, and any resemblance to actual events or
locales or persons, living or dead, is entirely coincidental.

No part of this publication may be reproduced, stored in a retrieval system,
or transmitted in any form or by any means, electronic, mechanical, photocopying,
recording, or otherwise, without written permission of the publisher. For
information regarding permission, write to Aladdin Paperbacks, an imprint of
Simon & Schuster Children's Publishing Division, 1230 Avenue of the Americas,
New York, NY 10020.

ISBN 978-0-545-23503-7

Copyright © 2010 by Lisa Schroeder. All rights reserved.
Published by Scholastic Inc., 557 Broadway, New York, NY 10012,
by arrangement with Aladdin Paperbacks, an imprint of Simon & Schuster
Children's Publishing Division. SCHOLASTIC and associated logos are
trademarks and/or registered trademarks of Scholastic Inc.

12 11 10   14 15/0

Printed in the U.S.A.   40

First Scholastic printing, February 2010

Designed by Karin Paprocki
The text of this book was set in MrsEaves.

For my sweet brother, Jim

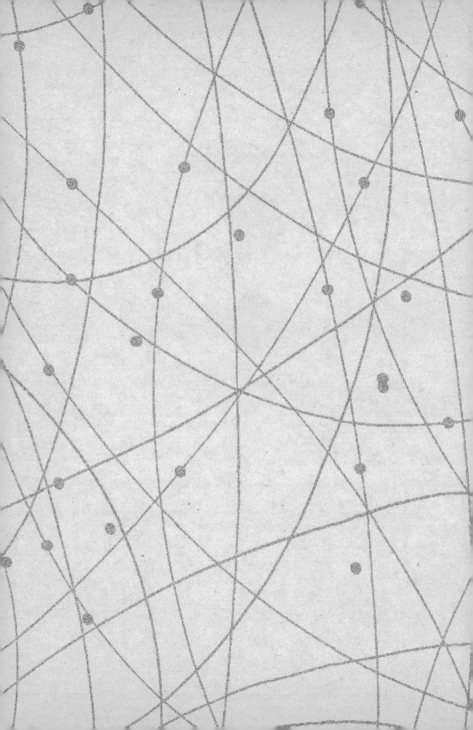

acknowledgments

A heartfelt thanks to Sara Crowe for loving this book from the start. To Alyson Heller and the team at Aladdin, thank you for your hard work to help make this book what I hope will be a delectable treat for those who read it. Lisa Madigan and Lindsey Leavitt, I owe you a lifetime of cupcakes for giving me your love, support, and writerly wisdom at just the right times. To Scott, Sam, and Grant, thanks as always for everything. Now we have a good excuse to eat lots of cupcakes. Be glad I didn't write a book about cucumbers.

It's Raining Cupcakes

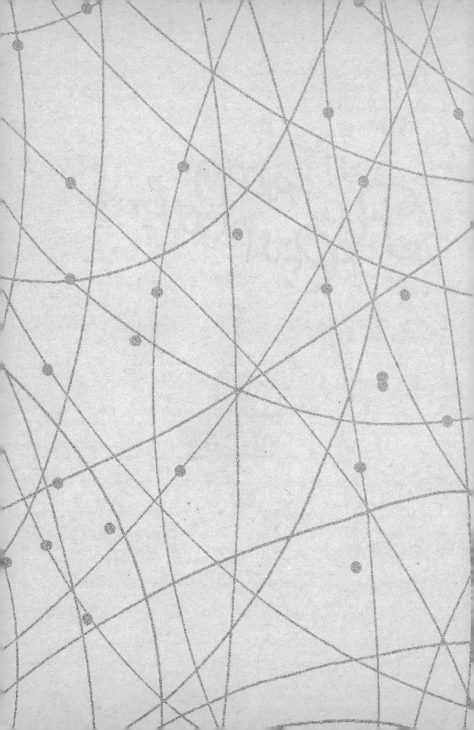

Chapter 1

red velvet cupcakes
A CLASSIC THAT NEVER
LETS YOU DOWN

The whole cupcake thing started a couple of years ago, on my tenth birthday. My mom tried a recipe for red velvet cupcakes with buttercream frosting. She said, "Isabel, this recipe comes from a very famous cupcake shop in New York City called St. Valentine's Cupcakes. We're going to make these cupcakes for your party!"

Now, my mother isn't big on birthday parties. Since I was six, I've pretty much planned my own party, from the handmade invitations we deliver right down to the candy we put in the goodie bags.

But baking is what Mom loves. And it's the one thing we've liked doing together. She told me once there's something really satisfying about throwing stuff into a bowl and watching a mess turn into something wonderful. And she's right. There is.

That year for my birthday party, only four girls were coming for a sleepover: my best friend Sophie, plus two other girls from school. With such a small group, Mom thought cupcakes made more sense than a big cake.

Those cupcakes turned out delicious. Better than delicious. Amazingly fabulous. And from that day on, all Mom could talk about were cupcakes. Dad and I listened, because we were just glad she was talking about something. When she started talking about opening a cupcake shop, we listened and nodded our heads like it was the best idea ever. I don't think either of us *really* thought it was the best idea ever. But after years of trying odd jobs here and there, and complaining about how they were too easy or too hard, too weird or too boring, too right or too wrong, it was nice to hear good stuff for a change.

The talking turned into more than talking last year, when she convinced Dad to buy an old Laundromat with an apartment upstairs. It's called a walk-up apartment, and they're more common in big cities, like New York City or Chicago, than the town I live in: Willow, Oregon, population 39,257.

Mom didn't see a Laundromat. She saw a cute cupcake shop where she could make cupcakes every day and finally be happy. I think that's what she saw. I'll admit, I didn't see that at first.

We moved into the apartment right away, even though the cupcake shop wouldn't be ready for a while. Mom and Dad took out a loan and hired a contractor to do the work downstairs.

As a bunch of big, burly guys hauled the washing machines out of the building and into a large truck, I asked Mom, "Where will they go to wash their clothes now?"

"Who?" she asked.

"The people who brought their baskets of dirty

laundry here every week. Where will they go?"

She looked at me like I had a washing machine for a head. "Well, I don't know, Isabel. But it really doesn't matter, does it? I'm sure there are other Laundromats in town."

"Seems like running a Laundromat, where people wash their own clothes, would be a lot easier than running a cupcake shop, where *you* have to bake all the cupcakes."

Mom sighed. "I don't want a Laundromat. Who would want a Laundromat? I want to bake cupcakes. I want people to walk into my warm, wonderful shop and tell me how much they love my cupcakes. Besides, it won't just be me doing all the baking. Grandma's going to help. And you can even help sometimes."

Maybe it was the fact that this new adventure had forced me to move away from my best friend, Sophie, who'd lived right next door. Maybe it was the fact that my mother expected me to help without even asking if I wanted to. Or maybe, deep down inside, I didn't think Mom would be able to pull off this cupcake thing. All I know is I still wasn't sold.

"But I don't get it, Mom. Do you really think people

are going to want to eat cupcakes in a place where they used to wash their dirty, stinky socks?"

This time she looked at me like she wanted to shove a dirty, stinky sock into my mouth. "Isabel, Dad assures me we can turn it into an adorable cupcake shop. Let's not look back at what's been, but look ahead to what might be. Okay?"

Was that my mother talking? I must have given her a funny look, because she shrugged and said, "I heard it on TV. I thought it sounded good."

While Mom and Dad were busy getting the shop ready and organizing the apartment, I'd ride my bike up to the public library for something to do. I'd sit at a table right next to the travel section and read books about the places I wanted to visit someday.

See, my aunt Christy is a flight attendant. She sends me cool postcards from all over the world. When she came to visit last time, I asked her if she liked her job, and she said she doesn't just like it, she *loves* it. She gets to meet interesting people and see fascinating places. I asked her if she thought I could be a flight attendant someday, and she smiled real big and said, "You would make a fantastic flight attendant, my dear Isabel."

As I read those books, I'd dream of taking a cable car ride through San Francisco, or watching a Broadway play in New York City, or eating pastries outside a cute little café in Paris. Compared to those places, our town of Willow seemed about as interesting as dry toast.

I'd never been anywhere outside the state of Oregon. Grandma calls me a native Oregonian, like it's something to be proud of. What's there to be proud of? The fact that I own three different hooded coats, because it's the best way to be ready when the sky decides to open up and pour?

A couple of days after we moved in, Dad and I went to the dollar store because he needed to buy some clipboards and pads of paper for him and Mom. He said there was a lot to do in the coming days, and he wanted to help Mom stay organized. Dad is good at making lists. Not just good. He's the King of Lists. He usually scribbles them on whatever he can find—the back of an envelope, a corner of the newspaper, a piece of toilet paper. I thought it was sweet how he wanted to help Mom out and buy real paper for a change.

While he scoured the store for list-making supplies, I wandered down the aisles with a single dollar bill, looking for something interesting to buy. In a bin next to dollhouse-size bottles of shampoo and conditioner were a bunch of white plastic wallets with tiny pictures of suitcases on them. I picked one up and opened it. A piece of paper was stuck inside that said, "Passport Holder."

I imagined a girl like me eating a bowl of soup at a restaurant in Athens, Greece. Suddenly she bumps the bowl, and soup spills all over the table. She gasps when she notices her passport is sitting there on the table. But then she breathes a sigh of relief, because she remembers she bought a passport holder at the dollar store to keep her passport safe. She opens it and finds the passport perfectly soup free.

Of course I had to buy it. Even if I didn't have a passport to put inside the passport holder.

When I got home, I put little pieces of paper inside it to make a mini-notebook. I carried it around with me everywhere, and whenever I had a thought about traveling, I wrote it down. This is what I wrote the first day:

I want to go
on many journeys.
I want to meet interesting people
and experience new things.
—Isabel Browning

As I wrote that in my passport-holder-turned-note-book, I realized something important. If I ever wanted to get past the Oregon-Idaho border, I needed to make a plan. A fantastic, incredible, big moneymaking plan.

And I thought turning a Laundromat into a cupcake shop was hard.

Chapter 2

strawberry
lemonade cupcakes

THE PERFECT PICK-ME-UP

It says 'The Bleachorama,'" Sophie said, when she finally came over for a visit the day after the Fourth of July. We were standing in front of our building, piles of sheetrock and boards on the sidewalk, and guys carrying tools at every turn.

They hadn't taken the tacky neon sign down yet. If I was in charge, it would have been the first to go.

"Mom's getting a new one made. Guess what she's calling the shop?"

"Caroline's Cupcakes?" Sophie asked.

I shook my head. A worker carrying a can of cream soda walked by. I waved at him. He waved back.

"Cupcakes R Us?"

I shook my head again. "You'll never guess. So I'll just tell you. It's Raining Cupcakes."

"It's Raining Cupcakes?" she asked. "That's the name?"

"Yep. You know, 'cause it's almost always raining in Willow. Now it'll be raining cupcakes."

"Riiiight. Okay, show me your room. Can we take the fire escape?"

"Sophie, are you kidding? Dad would kill me. We have to go the normal way."

"Have you met Stan?" she asked, pointing to the sign STAN'S BARBER SHOP on the building next door to ours.

"Yeah. He's round and bald and has a big, bushy mustache. And he's really nice."

Stan and his wife live upstairs, in an apartment down the hall from us. The first time I met him, I knew I'd like him. He smells like shaving cream, and he loves to tell knock-knock jokes. When I told him my name, he told me this one:

"Knock-knock."

"Who's there?"

"Isabel."

"Isabel who?"

"Isabel out of order? I had to knock!"

I led Sophie between the two storefronts to a door. Behind the door is a little room that doesn't hold much of anything except mailboxes along one wall and the stairs that take us up to the apartments. Dad told me they constructed buildings like ours to make the most out of the space, and to allow people other than the owners of the shops to rent the apartments above them.

"Then why did we move?" I'd asked him. "We could have stayed where we were and rented the apartment out to someone else."

He just smiled and said, "Your mom liked the idea of walking to work."

Living at work is more like it, I thought.

As Sophie and I walked up the old, creaky stairs,

she whispered, "Chickarita, this place is majorly cool."

We got to the top and turned to the right. As we approached the door, we heard Mom humming a tune, happy as a sparrow on a spring day.

"Wow, guess cupcakes really do make her happy," Sophie said.

"For now." I didn't have to say any more. Sophie knew. My mom has more moods than there are sparrows in Oregon, and that's a lot.

When Sophie and I walked into the tiny family room, I noticed it still didn't feel like home. It felt like someone else's place with our worn-out furniture and some of the equipment Mom had bought for the bakery.

The fan hummed in the corner, adding more noise to the room than cool air. Dad swore we'd get an air conditioner for the window as soon as we could afford it. Until then, during the hot months of July and August, we'd have to dream of cold December days and drink lots of ice-cold drinks.

Mom sat in the old, tan La-Z-Boy, with a cookbook in her lap and a whole pile of them stacked beside her on the end table. "Girls, do you think pineapple cupcakes would be good?" she asked.

"My mom and I make pineapple upside-down cake all the time," Sophie said. "My little brother thinks it's disgusting. But it's my dad's favorite."

"Oh, you're right," Mom said. "I don't think Isabel and I have ever baked pineapple upside-down cake. Have we, Is?" I shook my head. "Hmmm, I wonder why. Anyway, they wouldn't be quite the same, but I bet they'd still be good. I'm adding it to the list."

"How many flavors are you up to?" I asked, walking toward the kitchen. "Hey Soph, you want a root beer?"

She gave me a nod and followed.

"Seven," Mom said. "I figure I need at least eight to start with. Of course, we'll have to come up with new ones as we go along. Fun, exciting flavors will keep people coming back. Isabel, you can help me come up with catchy little sayings to go with them. You're good at that kind of thing."

"Sure," I said. "I can do that." I reached into the fridge, grabbed two cans of root beer (my favorite), and handed one to Sophie.

"How about if you have a flavor of the month?" Sophie said, popping the top. "You know, like the ice cream shops have?"

Mom gave a little squeal. "Sophie, that's brilliant! Flavor of the month. Why didn't I think of that? So, what should our first month's flavor be?"

"When are you opening?" asked Sophie as she sat down on the plaid couch.

"Should be August fifteenth," Mom said. "They're working fast and furious down there to make it happen."

"Hottest month of the year," I said. "Maybe something with 'cool' in the title. Cool as a Cucumber?"

"Ewwww," they said at the same time.

I laughed. "Okay, maybe not." I took a drink of my root beer. "What about root beer cupcakes? Or iced tea?"

"I know!" Sophie said. "Strawberry lemonade! Nothing says summer like strawberry lemonade."

Mom clapped her hands together, "Yes! I can cut up some strawberries and add a splash of lemon. Perfect! Sophie, you're a genius."

Sophie hadn't even been there five minutes and my

mom had already called her brilliant and a genius. But that's Sophie for you.

Mom set the cookbook down and jumped up. "I think I'll go buy the ingredients right now and make some. And I need some new cupcake pans, since the ones I ordered for the bakery are too large and don't fit in the oven up here. If you two are still around, you want to help me? It'll be fun. We haven't baked together in a while, with the move and everything."

I had to admit, strawberry lemonade cupcakes sounded pretty good to me. "Sure, Mom. We'll probably be here."

"Okay. If you need anything, your dad is downstairs, going over some things with the contractor. I won't be gone long."

After she left, Sophie said, "Wow, she really *is* happy."

I nodded. "She's never been this excited about anything. I just hope it lasts."

"Okay," Sophie said, pulling on my arm, "show me your room!"

"Close your eyes," I said.

"What?"

"Come on, just do it. I'll lead you. Trust me."

She put her hands over her eyes while I gently pulled her behind me down the hallway and into my room.

"Okay, you can open them."

Now it was her turn to squeal. "Isabel, it's totally purplicious! How come you didn't tell me?"

"'Cause I wanted to surprise you," I said. "Isn't it just so cool?"

We stood there, admiring the pretty walls, partially covered with posters of the places I dreamed of visiting: the Space Needle in Seattle, Niagara Falls in New York, the Dover Castle in England, the Swiss Alps in Switzerland, and lots more.

The person who lived in the apartment before us had painted the bathroom and the two bedrooms really bright colors. Mom and Dad's room was turquoise. The bathroom was orange. And my room was purplicious, as Sophie and I liked to say. Our favorite color.

I walked across the room and turned on the fan. Sophie chugged the rest of her root beer, then did a belly flop on my freshly made bed. "Lucky girl. You get to have a cupcake shop where you can eat all the cupcakes you want *and* the most fabulous room I've ever seen."

I set my can on the nightstand and sat down beside her. "I guess. I miss the old neighborhood, though." I reached over and grabbed her hand and squeezed it. "I miss you, Sophie Bird."

She laughed and rolled over. "You haven't called me that in a long time. Oh my gosh, remember that day?"

How could I forget? We'd climbed a huge oak tree at the park down the street from our duplex. I stopped at about the fifth branch up because it was high enough for me. But not Sophie. She wanted to go higher. She went so high, I yelled up at her, "What do you think you are, a bird?"

It took her forever to get down. At one point I thought I was going to have to get help. But she did it. She's amazing that way. She accomplishes whatever she sets her mind to.

In fourth grade she'd wanted a puppy. Her mom was allergic, so she'd always said no when Sophie asked. But Sophie decided she couldn't live without a dog any longer, and researched and researched until she found a great breed that doesn't shed and is hypoallergenic. Within six months, she had her very own Havanese puppy named Daisy.

In fifth grade she decided she wanted to be the school's spelling bee champion. She studied words from the dictionary every day for months. It didn't surprise me at all when she won and went on to the state championship.

In sixth grade she ran for class president. She wrote speeches, made posters, and went on campaign walks down the hallway, shaking people's hands. They said she won by a landslide.

As I sat there with her, I wondered what she would accomplish in seventh grade. And I thought maybe, just maybe, I could get her to help *me* accomplish something.

> *I envy birds who can fly.*
> *I want to fly too.*
> *On an airplane.*
> *—IB*

Chapter 3

peanut butter and jelly cupcakes

KIDS GO WILD OVER THESE

I need to find a way to make some money," I told Sophie as she picked up a *National Geographic* from my nightstand. Mr. Nelson, my sixth-grade social studies teacher, had given it to me.

"Won't your mom pay you for working in the cupcake shop?"

"I don't think so. They have to pay back the loan

they've taken out, and there won't be a lot of money left over. Besides, I'm not old enough to work, so it's not *really* working, you know? And I bet it won't be very often. I mean, I have school. I have a life!"

"And turtles!" Sophie said, as she picked up one of my many stuffed turtles that lay at the end of my bed. "You can't bake cupcakes, Chickarita. The turtles need you!"

I snatched the turtle from her hands. "Yeah, to save them from the turtle haters of the world like you!"

My grandma got me a stuffed turtle for my fifth birthday. I sort of became obsessed with them. She still gets me one every year, so now I have, like, a whole army of turtles.

Sophie sat up and tossed the magazine back where she found it. "Okay. So what do you need the money for?"

I bit my lip. I wasn't sure if I should tell her. What if she didn't understand?

"Don't laugh, okay? I want to go on a trip. It's so pathetic that I've never been anywhere outside of Oregon!"

She sat up straighter. "Ooh, a trip! How fun! Maybe you can go to Disneyland. I had so much fun when we went a few years ago. Okay, so Hayden screamed like his arm was being cut off at the sight of Mickey or Goofy, or any of the other characters, but still. It was a blast."

I decided not to tell her that a trip to an amusement park wasn't really what I had in mind. She kept talking. "Well, I know Mrs. Canova across the street from us is looking for a mother's helper to watch her three-year-old twins. She's doing cooking shows and selling kitchen tools in people's homes a couple of nights a week. She wants someone to come a few hours a day and watch the boys while she works in her office, making calls and doing computer work. She asked me to do it, but I'm leaving for camp in a few days."

I felt my stomach tighten up. I'd forgotten she was going to camp. "How long are you going to be gone?"

"Three weeks. Well, camp is for two weeks, but after Mom and Dad pick me up, we're going to the Grand Canyon for vacation."

My stomach got even tighter. "You get to see the Grand Canyon?"

She stood up and stretched, her arms clasped above her head. She reached to the right just slightly, reminding me of a tall, lean ballerina.

"Yeah. If I survive the car ride. Hayden's latest obsession is the solar system. The whole way there, I'll have to listen to him spout off facts about Saturn and Mars and every other planet in the galaxy. I don't get it. Who cares about planets that are millions of miles away?"

"Girls," Mom called from the other room, "I'm back. Want to come help make the cupcakes?"

I looked at Sophie and shrugged. "You want to?"

She started walking toward the door. "Sure. But wait. Are you gonna go see Mrs. Canova?"

"Yeah, I probably will, if Mom and Dad say it's okay. Little kids aren't my most favorite thing in the world, but how hard can it be?"

She laughed and threw her arm around me as we walked down the hall. "Oh, sure. A piece of cake. Or should I say, cupcake?"

❋ ❋ ❋

I got the job and started a couple of days later. I think scrubbing floors with a toothbrush would have been easier than babysitting two toddler boys.

"No, Lucas, don't—" But I was too late. The bowl of water he'd been using to dip his paintbrush in was now all over the kitchen floor. Frustrated that his blue blob looked nothing like a stegosaurus, he had grabbed the bowl and dumped its contents.

Logan sat in his chair, paintbrush out like a sword drawn for battle, little chuckles coming from his mouth as he said, "Dat's funny."

The chuckles turned into a full-blown laugh as they watched me on my hands and knees, trying to sop up the water with a big wad of paper towels.

"It's not funny," I told them. "We have to be careful when we're painting. Very, very careful. You understand, Lucas?"

Lucas nodded his head, then grabbed his paintbrush and painted across the kitchen table. "Keep paint on paper."

Knowing that paint on a table is much worse than water on a floor, I tried to jump up and clean it before it dried. Normally that would have been fine, except the floor was slippery, so my flip-flops couldn't get a firm grip, and I ended up back on the floor. Total face plant.

Lucas and Logan threw their paintbrushes in the air like confetti to celebrate the occasion, and laughed until they cried.

Me? I just cried.

When I got home, a pretty pink sign with elegant black lettering greeted me.

It's Raining Cupcakes

I ran up the stairs, excited to tell Mom how great the sign looked. After I turned the corner when I reached the top of the stairs, I ran right into Stan, carrying suitcases in both hands.

"Isabel," he said, laughing. "You in a hurry?"

"Oh, sorry. Hey, are you going somewhere?"

"Just getting them out of storage. We don't leave for another week. Judy and I are going to jolly old England."

My heart leaped at the thought. "You're going to England? What part?"

"The northeastern part to start with. County Durham, North Yorkshire, and Northumberland."

"You'll get to see Durham Castle! And the Durham Cathedral!"

He chuckled. "Have you been there, Isabel?"

I shook my head. "I just read a lot."

He nodded like he understood. "Well, you probably know more about the place than I do. I'm not much into traveling. More of a homebody myself."

"Then why are you going?"

He smiled. "Because I have a wife who has wanted to go to England for years. I surprised her and bought tickets for an anniversary gift. Our thirtieth is coming up in a couple of weeks. Anyway, I'll send you a postcard, how's that?"

"I'd love that. Wait, are you closing your barber shop while you're gone?"

He nodded. "I figure with all the construction going on, it's for the best anyway."

The way he said it made me feel funny. Was he

angry that we had moved in and things were changing in the neighborhood? Maybe he had liked having a Laundromat next door. And maybe he didn't *like* cupcakes.

He must have read my mind. "No worries, though. You're sprucing up the neighborhood. I bet my business increases tenfold thanks to you."

That reminded me of something I'd been wondering about. "Hey, who lives in the third apartment up here? I haven't seen anyone else around."

"That'd be Lana. She's away on a trip herself. To visit family, I believe. Can't remember when she's due back. But anyway, you'll like her. She's a real nice gal."

I smiled. "See ya later, Stan. Have fun packing."

"Knock-knock," he said.

"Who's there?"

"Stan."

"Stan who?"

"Stan back! I think I'm going to sneeze!"

Ha, more like, Stan gets to go to England and Isabel doesn't. No fair!

I pulled my passport book out of my back pocket, along with the tiny pencil I carried, and wrote:

Queens live in castles.
I'd love to visit a castle
and feel like a queen
for a day.
—IB

When I walked into our apartment, a gray, smoky haze greeted me. And the smell! It was like when cheese from the pizza drips onto the bottom of the oven and burns, only worse.

"Mom? Dad?"

"In here!" Dad yelled.

He was in the kitchen, using a towel to wave smoke away from a cupcake pan.

"What happened? Where's Mom?"

"She's in her room. Go open all the windows and then see if she's all right."

I went around the apartment and opened every window. It was sunny and warm outside—not much of a breeze—so it didn't help a whole lot.

When I got to her bedroom, I found Mom sitting on her bed, staring out the window. I sat down next to her.

My stomach felt funny. Nervous. Mom let things get to her so easily. Little things that most people can just laugh off. But not my mother. I'd learned over the years that talking to her when she was upset about something was like that game where you walk across the yard with an egg on your spoon, the whole time trying not to drop the egg. As I sat next to her, my mind whispered, *Careful, be careful, step slooowly*.

I thought of the time she had planted a garden a few years ago at our duplex. She was excited about growing her own carrots, radishes, and tomatoes. Things seemed to be going along pretty well. The plants started growing, and we could see the first signs of some yummy vegetables. But then one morning she woke up and discovered a bunch of gopher holes. Dad said they could try traps, but she wasn't interested. She just gave up. Said she wasn't meant to be a farmer, and that's why we have grocery stores anyway. So while the moles had a party in our backyard, Mom spent the rest of the day in her room.

Grandma told me one time that Mom is missing the gumption gene. Of course I had no idea what gumption was. It sounded to me like some kind of terrible soup. When I told Grandma that, she laughed and explained that it means spirit or spunk. When things don't go quite right, Mom's solution is to just give up.

"Mom?" I asked.

She didn't answer.

"Are you all right? Did you burn yourself or anything?"

She shook her head and sighed. "I'm fine. Just not cut out to make cupcakes."

I turned and faced her. "Mom, everyone burns things. We put something in the oven and we forget. Remember that one time I burnt a batch of snickerdoodles? I felt so bad, and you told me not to worry, because it was just one batch and we still had plenty of dough to make lots of cookies for the bake sale. Now I'm telling you, don't worry! You're the best baker I know. Come on. Cheer up! The sign is *so* beautiful. It made me excited when I saw it. Didn't it make you excited?"

She turned to face me. Her mousy brown hair was kind of messed up and her green eyes looked sad.

But for a moment, there was a little sparkle in them. "It is beautiful, isn't it?"

"Yes! So be happy, okay? Now I'm going to make dinner for us tonight. You rest if you want to, but I'm coming to get you in thirty minutes."

"Thanks, Is."

I gave her a quick hug before I re-entered the smoke zone.

"Is she okay?" Dad asked. He was sitting on the couch, checking things off the list on his clipboard.

"Yeah. I think she's just worried. I mean, it's a scary thing, opening a new business, right?"

Dad looked at me. He tried to smile, but the wrinkles in his forehead told me he was worried too. "You're right. It's scary for anyone. She'll be fine. We just need to stay positive even when she worries."

"I'm going to make dinner. Tacos all right?"

He turned the TV on and started flipping through the channels. "Sounds good," he said. "Thanks, honey." When he came to a baseball game, he stopped. I could tell from the uniforms that the Red Sox were playing the Yankees. Dad's a huge Red Sox fan.

"Did you know Stan is going to England?" I asked

him as I leaned up against the back of the sofa behind where he sat. He turned and looked up at me for a second, and I noticed how tired he looked.

He'd been working long hours downstairs, helping to get the cupcake shop ready. During the school year, he taught high school math, but every summer he spent his time differently. One year he taught summer school. Another year he painted the inside and outside of our old duplex. This year he was helping to get the cupcake shop ready. As I thought about it, I realized the guy never stopped. Never took the time to rest. I know some people like to keep busy, and maybe it was his way of dealing with Mom and her stuff, but still, it just didn't seem right to me.

"Yeah," Dad said. "Stan told me. Sounds like a great trip."

"Dad, how come we never go anywhere? Isn't it just completely sad that I've never even been on an airplane?"

He reached over and patted my hand resting on the top of the sofa. "Sad? No. Disappointing? Maybe. When you get older, you can travel all you want, how's that?"

"Well, that's why I want to be a flight attendant. But really, do I have to wait that long?"

He gave a little grunt as one of the batters struck out. Then he looked back at me. "Didn't your aunt Christy say she'd take you on a trip when you turn sixteen?"

"That's four years, Dad. Four long years. How come we can't take a vacation? A real vacation? You need one! We could go to Florida or Mexico, or what about Australia?"

He laughed. "Australia? You've never even been out of Oregon and suddenly you want to see Australia?"

"I want to see everything! And anything! I'm so tired of Willow. Aren't you?"

He turned back to watch the game. "No," he said quietly. "This is our home, Isabel. We belong here."

We belong here? Or we're stuck here? I wanted to tell him there was a difference. But instead I went into the kitchen and made tacos. Just like I belonged there.

Chapter 4

chocolate coconut cupcakes

TASTE LIKE A MILLION BUCKS

J was a complete idiot and took the babysitting job without asking how much I'd get paid. When Mrs. Canova paid me on Friday for the two days I'd worked that week, she gave me thirty dollars. That was only fifteen dollars a day. Okay, I didn't actually work the whole day, just a half day. But still, I guess I'd expected a little more. It was hard work trying to keep up with those boys!

I was complaining to Sophie about it the day before she had to leave for camp, after I'd spent the afternoon repairing the damage caused by the dual cyclone known as Lucas and Logan. While I'd been doing the dishes after snack time, they'd decided to take the books off the bookshelf in their room and wipe the pages clean with the flushable wipes they found in the bathroom.

"Wipes are for your bottoms, not your books," I told them when I walked in and saw what they were doing.

They just laughed, like always.

"Well, think of it this way," Sophie said, trying to shove another sweatshirt into her already full suitcase. "By the end of the summer, you should have a few hundred bucks, right? That might be enough money to buy an airplane ticket."

"Yeah, right. If I want to go to Pocatello, Idaho."

I lay on her bed, looking at her bookshelf and the soccer and softball trophies she'd won over the years. Her parents had always encouraged her to try new things. She'd played sports, taken piano lessons, and participated in the summer children's theater program until now, when she was finally too old.

I'd never done any of those things. My mom thought sports were dangerous. We didn't have a piano. Or any instrument, for that matter. When I asked for a guitar one time, Mom said noise gave her bad headaches, as if she didn't think I could actually make the thing sound good.

As for the theater, I could never picture myself up on a stage. Sophie's good at that kind of thing. But not me. While she was gone, I'd stay home and read books, or watch soap operas, waiting for our antique clock to chime four o'clock. That was when Sophie would come home, and we'd play outside before dinner.

Now Sophie smacked her forehead with the palm of her hand in a very dramatic way, snapping me back to reality about my moneymaking dilemma. "Oh my gosh, Is, I have the perfect solution. I can't believe I almost forgot to tell you. Does your mom still get *Baker's Best* magazine?"

"I don't think so," I said. "At least, I haven't seen one lying around lately. Why?"

She reached over and opened the top drawer of her desk. I sat up as she handed me a magazine, open to a page that read BAKING CONTEST FOR KIDS AGES 9—14.

"A baking contest?" I asked her, my heart starting to pound inside my chest. "Are you going to enter?"

She nodded, and her eyes got really big. "Grand prize is a thousand dollars. But you have to come up with a recipe on your own. No one can help you. Not your mom, not your grandma, no one."

My eyes skimmed the rules. They were looking for a completely original dessert recipe. Each entry would be graded on easiness to prepare, uniqueness, presentation, and taste. All entries had to be postmarked by August 1, which wasn't that far away.

When I got to the bottom of the paragraph, I jumped off the bed. "Finalists will be flown to New York City along with one parent or guardian for a bake-off!" I yelled. "Sophie, we could go to New York! The Statue of Liberty. Metropolitan Museum of Art. Radio City Music Hall!"

"Does it say how many finalists there'll be?" she asked.

"No. But wouldn't it be fun if we both made it?"

She sat down on her suitcase, reached down, and flipped the latches closed. "It would be a blast." Then she pointed her finger at me. "As long as you know I'm in it to win."

I smiled. "What do you want the money so bad for, anyway?"

She stood up and took the suitcase off her bed, and then, with a loud grunt, dropped it on the floor. "The future. As for the present, I think I packed too much. I have to pack in case it's ninety degrees or forty. How come Oregon's weather is so unpredictable, anyway?"

"Wait a minute. What do you mean the future? Like college?"

She took the magazine from my hand and threw it on the bed. "Maybe. Come on. Time for you to go home so I can get my toiletries packed. Isn't that a stupid word? Toiletries? It makes it sound like the stuff comes from the toilet."

She walked me to the door, and I gave her a quick hug. "See you when you get back," I told her. "I'll be practicing recipes while you're gone."

"I should have waited and told you after camp," she said. "Now you have the unfair advantage. Especially since I'll only have a few days to make the deadline when I get home. I'll have to work fast."

"Hey, maybe while you're at camp, you'll come up with a new and improved s'more recipe."

"How can you improve the s'more? It's, like, chocolaty marshmallow perfection."

"Bye, Sophie Bird. See you in three."

"Bye, Chickarita. Be good."

I made a quick note in my passport book:

> *I've heard walking down a busy sidewalk in New York*
> *is like swimming in a sea of people.*
> *I love to swim and I love people,*
> *so of course I would love*
> *New York!*
> *—IB*

I hopped on my bicycle, my thoughts turning faster than the spokes underneath me. A trip to New York and a thousand dollars!

I knew I just had to win that baking contest. Even if it meant, for once, that something didn't go Sophie's way.

Chapter 5

carrot cake cupcakes

PETER RABBIT'S FAVORITE

When I got home, Grandma was there, helping Mom in the kitchen. The apartment smelled spicy, like cinnamon.

"Izzy!" Grandma said when I walked in. She was the only one who ever called me that. "Just in time to try our latest creation. After I get a hug, of course."

I wrapped my arms around her tiny waist and let

her squeeze me real tight, being careful not to bump her pink pillbox hat.

Grandma always wears a hat. Her closet has two long shelves with stacks of hatboxes piled high. Inside are hats with veils, hats with beads, hats with feathers, hats with sequins—just about any kind of hat you can imagine. My grandpa was in the hatmaking business for a long time, until hats went out of style. He moved on to other things, but he always had a soft spot for hats, and it made him happy when Grandma wore them. Even after he died a few years ago, she kept wearing them. Some of the hats she has are probably sixty years old, and she usually has a crazy story about each one. I never know if she's serious or just making it up.

"Nice outfit," I told her when I pulled away. Underneath her apron, I could see she had on a tailored white and pink pantsuit. Since she always wore a hat, she felt like she had to dress up to match.

"Thanks, cupcake," she said. "You're looking quite ducky yourself."

"Ducky" is Grandma's favorite word. Says it all the time. Drives Mom crazy.

"This hat," she continued, "is just like one the First Lady Jackie Kennedy wore that sad, sad day her husband died. I met Jackie Kennedy once, many years ago, at a fundraising dinner, did you know that? Lovely lady. We exchanged the usual pleasantries, then she leaned in to whisper in my ear. Why, my heart started racing, because I thought she was going to tell me some big secret. But you know what she said?" She paused to give a little giggle. "She told me that I had a smudge of lipstick on my teeth. Wasn't that kind of her? It really felt like we had been friends forever."

I nodded like I always did when she started talking about people like that. Then my eyes traveled around the kitchen. A stack of dirty bowls sat next to the sink. About eight trays of cupcakes, most with one missing, were scattered across the gray Formica countertops. "Doing a little baking, huh?"

"Oh yes. We've been perfecting one of our eight flavors. Carrot cake with cream-cheese frosting. Want to try the latest batch? We just frosted them."

I shrugged. I didn't really *like* carrot cake. "No, thanks. Are you sure you want carrot cake as one of the eight? I mean, is anyone really going to pick carrots over chocolate?"

The whole time Grandma and I had been having this exchange, Mom stood there, not saying anything. But as soon as I said that, she snapped out of her trance, throwing her towel on the counter. "She's right. She's absolutely right! What are we doing? We keep trying and trying to get this recipe right, when it shouldn't even be one of the eight flavors. It's boring. Vegetables are boring! We can't do carrot cake. We can't, Mom. We need to find something better."

Grandma wrapped her arm around Mom's shoulders and started leading her out of the kitchen. "Why don't you go take a rest? We've been on our feet all afternoon. Izzy and I will clean up in here. We can try again tomorrow."

"Wait!" I said. "Mom, before you go, I have the best news. Sophie told me about a contest in *Baker's Best* magazine. It's a baking contest for kids, ages nine to fourteen. We're both going to enter. The grand prize is a thousand dollars!"

They both turned around and looked at me,

Mom's eyes much brighter. "A baking contest? Will the finalists be on TV?"

"Um, I'm not sure. Anyway, I have to come up with a recipe and enter by the first of August. And the finalists are flown to New York City. Can you believe that? New York!"

"Oh, Isabel, you should come up with a cupcake recipe. If you make it into the finals, it could be great advertising for our little cupcake shop. We could even feature your cupcake—Isabel's cupcake—as one of the flavors of the month."

I looked over at Grandma. She just smiled, not saying anything. It felt like my heart had jumped up into my throat.

I tried to choose my words carefully, so I wouldn't upset her. "But Mom, cupcakes are your thing. Why can't I do my own thing? Besides, if I make cupcakes, they'll think you helped me with the recipe."

The corners of her lips turned down just slightly. "If you tell them you came up with it yourself, they'll believe you. Please, Isabel? This could be a chance for us to show the country our great little shop here. What does it matter what kind of recipe you enter, anyway? As long as you're in the finals, right?" She smiled again. "Oh, this is going to be great. I can't wait to see what kind of cupcake recipe you come up with. All those times we've baked together will come in handy now, won't they?"

And with that, they turned and walked toward Mom's bedroom.

I went to the sink, put the stopper in the drain, and turned the water on full blast. I threw beaters, scrapers, and silverware into the water, creating splash after angry splash.

How dare she tell me what to bake for the contest! Why was everything about *her*? Couldn't she think of *me* just once? What a stupid idea. They'd call me a cheater for sure. I didn't care what she said. I wasn't doing it.

Grandma came back in and stood beside me at the sink. She reached over and turned the water off. I hadn't noticed that the water in the sink was about to overflow. "You didn't add soap," she said softly.

I reached under the sink, grabbed the bottle of dishwashing soap, and squirted a bunch into the sink. "There. Now we have soap."

She rolled up her sleeve, stuck her hand in the water, and stirred the water hard. Bubbles rose to the surface. Then she turned and looked at me, her eyes soft and warm, like a blanket you reach for when you want to curl up and read a book.

"I know it must be hard, honey. You had to move. Your mother is stressed about getting this business off the ground. Your dad is busy working downstairs. All I can say is, follow your heart. Think about it, and do what your heart tells you to do. You have a good heart, I know that as sure as I know your grandpa loved hats."

Well, my heart sure didn't *feel* very good. "Grandma, I thought this was all going to make her happy. I mean, it's been me and Dad walking on eggshells around her for so long, and then, with this cupcake idea, she was finally thinking about something besides her problems for once. I thought things were going to be different. Better, you know?"

I blinked real fast, trying to keep my eyes from getting teary.

She gave me a squeeze, her wet hand cool on my shoulder. "You are an amazing girl, Izzy. I'm sorry it's so hard for you sometimes, but your mother loves you very much. Thank goodness she has you, honey. And you know, I think deep down she is happy. We just can't see it right now because of all the other stuff she's feeling too. It's stressful right now, but it'll get better. So try not to worry, okay?"

Easy for her to say. She didn't have to live with Mom.

While Grandma went to work washing the dishes in the sink, I walked over to a pan of cupcakes, ready to change the subject. I might like parties, but pity parties aren't my idea of a good time.

"What are we supposed to do with all these cupcakes?" I asked.

She shrugged her shoulders and smiled. "Those are the rejects. They weren't quite moist enough. They may not have had enough oil in them. Or she may have overmixed them. I'm not really sure. In any event, you can throw them away. The good batch is over there."

I followed her pointed finger to a plate of cute little cupcakes set aside, all nicely frosted, with two sliced almonds crisscrossed in the center of each.

"I'm going to go see if Stan and his wife are

around. Maybe they'll take some of these. We can't eat them all."

"That's a ducky idea, Izzy. I'm sure they'll appreciate that."

I walked down the hall to Stan's apartment and knocked, but nobody answered. Wondering if they'd already left for their trip, I went down the stairs and out the door, to see if the barber shop was open.

I hadn't been inside his shop before. There were two stations with big, black swivel chairs in front of mirrors along the right side of the shop. Along the back wall was a sink with a chair in front of it, and a shelf of shampoos and other products sitting above the sink. Up front, by the large picture window, sat a row of chairs with a coffee table in front of them, piled high with magazines. Two old guys sat there, reading the newspaper.

Stan was cutting a kid's hair, while the kid's dad stood beside him, watching.

"Well, Isabel, how nice to see you," Stan said, holding his scissors up in the air. "Need a trim?"

Without thinking, I reached up and touched my straight, short brown hair. Did it look like I needed a trim? Wasn't a barber just for men? "No, thanks. I'm good. I actually brought you some of my mom's cupcakes. We're doing a lot of baking and sampling, and one family can only eat so many, you know?"

"Pass them out," he said, waving the scissors around. "Except for Phillip here. He needs to wait until he's done. Otherwise he'll be picking hairs out of his food right and left. And it won't be the chef's fault."

By now the two men had set their newspapers down. They each took a cupcake and thanked me.

The dad standing next to his son took two. "I'll hold Phillip's until he's done."

"Well, land sakes," I heard from behind me. "This is one doggone good cupcake. You make these, miss?"

I turned around. One of the men was wiping frosting from his top lip, using his finger. I realized I should have brought napkins. Cupcakes can be messy.

"No. My mom. She's opening up a cupcake shop next door. The grand opening is August fifteenth. You should stop by. It's going to be really great."

"Delicious," the other man said. "Give your mother our compliments."

I felt my heart flutter in my chest. They liked

them! They liked the cupcakes. I couldn't wait to tell her. That'd give her a good boost of confidence.

Stan unsnapped the cape around the kid's neck, and the kid jumped out of the chair. "Can I have mine now?"

I started to warn him that it was carrot. He might be disappointed. But I didn't say anything, just bit my bottom lip and waited. Maybe the kid liked carrot cake. Maybe it was his absolute favorite. Yeah, right, and every kid begs to eat their brussels sprouts.

He bit into it, looked up at his dad, and said, with a mouthful of cupcake, "Mmmmmm. That's good."

"I know," agreed his dad. He looked at me. "They really are delicious. Thanks for sharing."

I smiled. "You're welcome."

Stan walked over and took two from the plate I was holding. "I'll take these home with me when I'm done here. The perfect dessert after supper tonight. Judy'll be thrilled."

"Good. Hey, when do you leave for your trip?"

"Tomorrow," he said. "We'll be back in a couple of weeks."

"Take lots of pictures. And don't forget to send me a postcard!"

"Okay, I will. See you when we get back."

I waved to everyone as I started to walk out.

Behind me, I heard Stan say, "Knock-knock."

The kid answered. "Who's there?"

"Phillip."

"Phillip who?"

"Phillip the gas tank, I'm running low."

I heard the boy laughing as the door closed behind me.

Back upstairs, Grandma had the kitchen just about cleaned up. Dad was standing there, talking to her. I handed him the plate, only half full now. "I took them down to the barber shop and passed them out. They loved them. I want to tell Mom."

Dad took hold of my arm as I started to leave, a nervous smile on his face. "Isabel, I just went in to see her. Please, don't say anything to upset her. This is a really hectic time for her."

Like he needed to tell me that. While I walked down the hall toward her room, I could feel my heart pounding in my chest. What would she say when I told her they liked the cupcakes? Would she even believe me? What if she brought up the contest again? Would I have to lie and tell her I would make cupcakes when I wasn't sure what I was going to make?

I took a quick right, went into my room, and shut the door. I'd tell her later. Or maybe it wasn't that big of a deal after all. Maybe I didn't even need to mention it.

I thought of Stan getting ready to go to England, and how I would have loved to be getting ready to go on a trip right about now.

Getting a postcard means
someone is thinking about you.
It's also like getting a little piece
of the place the person is visiting.
I love getting postcards.
When I travel someday,
I will send lots and lots
of postcards.
—IB

Chapter 6

banana cream pie cupcakes

WHEN IT'S HARD TO DECIDE WHICH DESSERT SOUNDS BEST

For the next couple of weeks, I spent most of my time either babysitting the twins or reading travel books in the library. And I thought about the baking contest. A lot. I couldn't figure out what to do. I didn't *want* to make cupcakes. But nothing else seemed quite right either. A pie sounded too difficult. Cookies were too ordinary. A cake was hardly different from cupcakes. I didn't know what to do.

It was fun to get a postcard from Stan in the mail. He sent me one with Durham Castle on the front. On the back he wrote:

> *Dear Isabel,*
> *We're having a jolly good time here. The weather's*
> *been truly grand. I miss everyone back home, however.*
> *Hope the cupcake shop is coming along splendidly.*
> *It's sure to be a smashing success.*
>
> *Cheerio, Stan*

I took it along with me to show the twins. They weren't impressed. "We want to swim!" Lucas said.

"We want to swim, we want to swim, we want to swim!" they chanted, marching around the family room.

We went outside to the backyard, only to find the kiddie pool completely empty.

"If I fill it up, the water's going to be *really cold*."

Lucas nodded his head hard, his blond curly hair flopping in his eyes. Those curls were my ticket to telling them apart. Logan didn't have nearly as many.

While Lucas nodded, Logan clapped his hands, like he'd never heard anything so exciting. *Really* cold water? Yay!

I dragged the hose over, stuck it in the swimming pool, and turned the faucet on. "Let's go inside and read books until it's full."

They didn't move.

"Come on, boys. It's going to take awhile."

They still didn't move.

"Please? If we're going to be sitting out here all afternoon, I want a book to look at." I had spotted a beautiful book about Colorado on their bookshelf the other day that I was dying to read.

The boys stood there, hypnotized by the water running from the hose into the pool. For once they weren't climbing something, spilling something, or tearing something apart.

"Okay, you stay here," I told them. "I'll be back in a second. But listen to me. Do not get into that pool. Do you understand me? If you get in, I'm throwing it away. You'll never, ever be able to swim again. You got that? DO NOT GET INTO THAT POOL."

"Okay," Logan said. Lucas nodded in agreement.

I ducked inside, kicked my flip-flops off, and ran to the front of the house where the living room was, all the while wondering how mothers of young children ever got anything accomplished. It seemed amazing that they weren't all walking around completely filthy from not having showered for months. Unless they were waking up at four a.m. every day and showering then. Maybe that was their trick.

I snatched up the book about Colorado, but as I did, my eyes couldn't help but scan for others. There were a lot. I took one called *50 Amazing Things to Do in Chicago*, and another one about Ireland, then hurried to the backyard.

When I got there, Mrs. Canova, or Sue as she insisted I call her, was standing there, arms crossed in that "I'm so appalled with you" way, as two completely dressed boys walked around inside the pool, kicking and splashing water at each other.

"Isabel?" Her eyes pierced mine.

I gulped. "Yes?"

"Did you leave them out here by themselves with a pool of water?"

"Well, it was filling up and—"

Her eyes narrowed even more as she stepped closer to me. "Did you, or did you not, leave them unattended with a pool of water?"

I looked down at my toes, the red nail polish I'd put on a month ago starting to chip away. Obviously, she already knew the answer to that question. She had found them outside, and I wasn't anywhere around.

"Yes," I whispered. "I'm sorry."

The boys' laughter filled the air. I listened to it, trying to make myself breathe. But I couldn't. It was like someone was standing on my chest, pressing harder and harder.

She reached over and took the books from my hands, then walked toward the sliding glass door. "I'm sure you understand, I can't have someone watching my children who displays such a lack of judgment. Do you know an accident can happen just like that?" She snapped her fingers. "I'm going to get my checkbook and pay you for the past five days. Please, stay here and watch them for another minute. And then your services will no longer be needed here."

After she left, I went over to the pool. I wanted

to cry, but I didn't want them to see me like that. I didn't want *her* to see me like that.

"Bye, boys. I have to go now."

"You throw it away now?" Lucas asked.

It made me smile. He asked like it was no big deal. Like it wouldn't matter to them one bit. Maybe they didn't even know what it meant.

"No. I'm the one being thrown away. I'll see you guys later. Be good for your mommy, okay?"

Sue came back and handed me my check. I apologized again, but she didn't say anything. She didn't have to. Her eyes said it all.

I knew I had to tell my parents. Not just tell them I wasn't working for Mrs. Canova anymore, but tell them *why*. If I made something up, like I quit or something, word would get back to them that I'd lied. Mom knew a lot of people in Willow, and she'd eventually find out, whether I told her or not.

Still, I didn't go home right away. I rode my bike to the library, the hot air stinging my eyes, making them water.

Okay, so maybe it wasn't the hot air.

For the first time in a long time, I didn't go to the travel section when I got to the library. I went to the cookbook section instead. It was time to come up with an idea. No more excuses.

"Isabel?" said a familiar voice as I was sitting at a table, looking at a lemon torte recipe.

I looked up.

"Mr. Nelson," I said, louder than I should have. "What are you doing here?"

Okay, stupid question. He was holding a stack of books. "Oh, you know, summer vacation is for reading, right?"

"Right." I smiled.

It was weird seeing my social studies teacher in shorts and a T-shirt. He looked different. Not like a teacher at all. More like an ordinary guy.

"Cookbooks?" he asked. "Taking up a new hobby?"

I shut the book. "I guess. I'm entering a baking contest. The finalists get to travel to New York City for a bake-off. Figured it might be my only chance to fly on an airplane and go somewhere interesting."

He sat down across from me. "Sounds like fun. My wife and I had a layover there on our way to Germany last summer. Stayed a couple of days so we could take in a Broadway play. It's an amazing city. All the people there? I don't think there's any place like it." His eyes smiled at me. "You'd probably love it there, Isabel. Seems to me you're quite the people person."

I wasn't sure what to say to that. "What part of Germany did you go to?" I asked as I picked at an annoying hangnail on my thumb.

"Frankfurt, Berlin, Hamburg, Heidelberg. We went all over. It's a beautiful country. Didn't care for the food much. But everything else was fantastic."

"Where are you going this summer?" I asked.

He leaned back in his chair, tipping it off the floor a little. It was funny to see an adult do that. I always got in trouble for it at home. "We're going to Washington, D.C., in a couple of weeks."

I sighed. "I'd love to go there. I'd see the Capitol Building, the Washington Monument, and the National Museum of Natural History for sure."

He laughed. "Yep. We'll see all of those."

"You're so lucky. Sometimes I feel like I'll be stuck in Willow forever."

Mr. Nelson tilted his head a little and looked at

me kind of funny. "Is everything all right at home, Isabel? Your parents doing okay?"

"Yeah. Just busy. We're getting ready to open a cupcake shop. You know where the Bleachorama used to be? The building is now the future home of It's Raining Cupcakes."

"Wow, that's exciting!" He stood up. "I'll have to stop by. I love cupcakes."

"That'd be great! We open on August fifteenth."

"Okay, Isabel, I need to get going. But I'll try to come by for the grand opening. And good luck with that contest. Are you going to make cupcakes?"

I shrugged. "I don't know yet."

"See ya later," he said.

"Say hi to the president for me!"

I pulled out my passport book and wrote in it:

> *Mr. Nelson made me love*
> *reading about other places.*
> *But reading about places*
> *and going places*
> *is just not the same.*
> *—IB*

I told Mom and Dad about the pool incident over a dinner of fried chicken and mashed potatoes. Mom didn't say a whole lot, just shook her head and pushed the food around on her plate.

"I feel bad, you know," I told them, wanting them to believe me. "I'd never want anything to happen to those little boys."

Dad took a drink of milk. "Drowning accidents can happen so fast. It probably just scared Sue something fierce. She's mad now. But she'll get over it. You apologized, right?"

"Yeah. But I don't think she believed me."

"It's okay," he said. "Look at it this way. We're getting close to opening day. Your mom could probably use some help with grocery shopping and testing some more recipes. Right, Caroline?"

"I suppose," she said, staring off into space.

"Mom, aren't you excited?" I asked. "You open in just a few more weeks! I've been telling everyone I see."

She stood up and took her plate to the counter. "Don't remind me. I'm not ready. I don't know why

I thought we could be ready by the fifteenth. It's too soon." She turned around. "David, I think we should wait. I think we should postpone the opening."

Dad stood up. "Honey, we're not going to wait. All the guys have been working so hard to have it ready. You just have cold feet. That's all. But Isabel getting fired is a blessing in disguise. She can help you with whatever you need—running errands, trying new recipes, advertising. Put her to work."

I sighed. There went the rest of my summer vacation.

While they continued their discussion, I snuck off to my room. I took a seat at my desk, feeling defeated about the entire day and thinking maybe I should just crawl into bed, when I saw two pieces of mail that had come for me.

The first was a postcard from my aunt, with a picture of the St. Louis Gateway Arch on the front.

Dear Isabel, I've been to St. Louis many times and never took the time to go up to the arch. It was fun!

The view from the top was incredible, and there's a cool museum inside about Lewis and Clark and their trip. Hope all is well with you. Is the cupcake shop coming along nicely? Love, Aunt Christy

The second was an envelope with Sophie's handwriting. I ripped it open and read.

Dear Is,

Camp sucks. I think I'm getting too old or something. Every activity seems lame, lamer, and lamest. I mean, canoeing on the lake isn't fun. It's work! Just ask my biceps. And archery? I used to be happy just getting the thing somewhere on the target. But now? No way. I want to hit the bull's-eye, baby! And of course, it's impossible. So I get frustrated and throw the thing on the ground. And then they yell at me. And then I cry. And then . . . well, you get the idea.

I want to come home. Next year, when my mom tells me I have to go, I'll just stay at your place and eat cupcakes for breakfast, lunch, and dinner for two weeks. Your parents won't mind, right?

What's going on in Willow? Working on your recipe? How are Thing 1 and Thing 2, otherwise known as Lucas and Logan? I don't know why I'm asking you questions. By the time you get this letter, I'll be on my way to the Grand Canyon, so you can't write me back. Can't wait to catch up when I get home.

Time for campfire. At least there won't be any singing tonight. Rachel's guitar somehow tragically lost all its strings. I wonder how that happened?

Campily yours,
Sophie

Thanks to Sophie, my stinky, stinkier, and stinkiest day ended on a happy note. I folded up the letter, tucked the envelope into a desk drawer, and crawled into bed underneath a blanket of turtles, figuring I'd better quit while I was ahead.

Chapter 7

coconut mango cupcakes

A TASTE OF THE TROPICS WITHOUT GETTING ON A PLANE

The next day, Mom and I were going through all the boxes that had been delivered, trying to figure out if we still needed to buy anything. Mom didn't say a word. She just emptied the boxes, took notes on her clipboard, and mumbled to herself every once in a while.

I wanted to tell her it'd be okay. I wanted her to know I thought it was great that she was trying to make a dream come true. I wanted to say *something* to make her feel better about everything. But I didn't know what to say. How many times had I wished I'd been born with the knowing-just-the-right-words-at-the-right-time gene, like Sophie had? More times than there are red-eyed tree frogs in the forests of Costa Rica, that's how many.

I decided maybe the best thing to do was to talk about something completely different. "Mom, where did you and Dad go on your honeymoon?"

She looked up from her clipboard with her left eyebrow raised. "What? Why?"

I shrugged. "You've never told me. And I'm curious."

"Well, we went to the Oregon coast. Stayed in a cottage for a week. It was very nice."

I peeled the packing tape off the top of the box in front of me. "You didn't go to Hawaii? Or Mexico? Or the Caribbean? Don't most people go to places like that?"

"Sometimes. And your father wanted to, I think.

I just couldn't do it. I couldn't envision myself getting on a plane."

My hands stopped moving, and my eyes looked up at her. "What do you mean?"

She stood up, a pair of wooden spoons in her hand. "I'm afraid, Isabel. I'm afraid to fly."

"You never told me that. How come you never told me?"

She shrugged. "I guess it never came up."

I could feel my heart racing. It didn't come up? All those times I'd rambled on about how I'd love to be like Aunt Christy, flying here and there and everywhere? All those times when I'd asked, "How come we never *go* anywhere?" Her response had always been brief and generic. "It's just not in the budget," or "Maybe someday we'll be able to."

Once again, it was all about *her.* The anger inside of me grew, like a cupcake expanding in the oven. I gritted my teeth and tried to sound as sweet as a chocolate chip cupcake. "Is that why we've never gone anywhere outside of Oregon?"

She made a checkmark on her clipboard. "Oh I don't know, Isabel. There are a lot of reasons.

Anyway, I know you want to travel. And you can blame me if you want to. But just think, you have the whole world to look forward to when you're older."

I started to respond to that with something I probably would have been sorry about later, but I didn't get the chance. There was a knock at the door.

I ran to open it before Mom had even taken a step. As the door flew open, Stan's big smile greeted me.

"You're home!"

"We just got in," he said. "And I wanted to bring you these." He held up a white box. "I thought you might enjoy one of my favorite treats from England. I bought these on the way to the airport and carried them with me the whole way. Judy thought I'd lost my mind. But jam tarts are delicious. And you were so kind to share your cupcakes with us."

I took the box from his hand. By now Mom was standing behind me. "Please, Stan, come in. But you'll have to excuse the mess. We're just going through the equipment for the shop. Not long until we open, you know."

He nodded as he stepped inside. "Yes, I know. August fifteenth, right? Those carrot cake cupcakes were wonderful, Caroline. Very moist and tasty. If your shop had been open, I'm sure Judy would have run downstairs and bought a half dozen more. I predict you are going to have more business than you can handle." He rubbed his belly. "And I predict my already large waistline will be getting even larger."

I looked at Mom, and she was all smiles.

"I got your postcard," I told him. "Thanks for sending it. Did you like the castle?"

"We sure did," he said. "That was actually one of many we saw. We had a great time. I'll have to show you the pictures one of these days."

"I'd love that," I said.

He looked around at the clutter on the floor. "Well, I don't want to keep you. Let me know how you like those tarts, Isabel."

He opened the door and stepped back into the hall.

"Knock-knock."

"Who's there?"

"Jam."

"Jam who?"

"Jamind? I'm trying to get outta here!"

"Bye, Stan," I said.

I skipped to the kitchen, carrying the box of tarts.

"Mom, come try a jam tart," I called, the anger I'd felt earlier now set aside on the cooling rack.

"No, thanks," she said. "I'm not really hungry." She paused, then called out, "Hey, I just remembered, how is that cupcake recipe coming along for the contest?"

I pulled a slightly squished but sweet-smelling jam tart from the box and took a bite. It was the most delicious thing I'd ever tasted.

"I'm, uh, still working on it."

"Do you need some help?"

That was pretty much the last thing I needed. "You can't help, Mom. That's one of the rules, remember?"

Besides, I thought, as I took another bite of the scrumptious tart, *I don't think you'll want to help me once you find out I'm submitting a jam tart recipe instead of a cupcake recipe.*

I pulled out my notebook.

Cupcakes are popular.
So is Disneyland.
Popular is good,
but it doesn't always mean
the best.
—IB

Chapter 8

root beer float cupcakes

A GOOD CHOICE EVERY TIME

At the library, I found hundreds of recipes for jam tarts. The basic recipe was pretty simple. But that didn't mean anything. I needed to make something different. Something all my own.

The tricky part was going to be baking jam tarts without Mom knowing what I was up to. If she found out, I knew her feelings would be hurt.

One afternoon I finally had the apartment to myself while Mom was running some errands and Dad was working downstairs. I'd just finished baking a batch of tarts that I'd made with some fresh lemon juice squeezed into the pastry crust. They were good, but still not something really different or totally fantastic.

I was racking my brain as I drank my second can of root beer, trying to figure out how I could make the world's greatest jam tarts, when I heard voices outside the apartment. As keys jingled, I heard Dad. And then Mom!

I grabbed the pan of tarts and ran to the family room, and without really thinking, I threw open the door that leads to the fire escape. And just like that, I was standing on the platform, looking down at the street below, with a pan of tarts in my hand.

I swear, sometimes I am not the sharpest knife in the drawer, as Mom likes to say. Why didn't I just go to my room and throw the pan under my bed? Now I was stuck out there until they left, unless I wanted to suddenly appear and have them ground me forever.

They'd told me probably a hundred times the fire escape was off-limits.

The door has glass in it, so I had to go to the very edge of the platform and stand against the railing to keep them from seeing me.

People scurried along the sidewalk below, completely unaware that I was standing above them. I put my hand over my mouth to keep myself from giggling at the thought of jam tarts suddenly raining from the sky. But the pastry in that batch was on the heavy side, and the last thing I wanted to do was to give someone a concussion. I could just picture someone going to the emergency room claiming they'd been hit on the head by a jam tart falling from the sky.

I stood there for a long time, listening to my parents chatting away inside, although I couldn't hear specifically what they were talking about. I took a bite of a tart and wondered if they might be worrying about me. I always left a note letting them know where I was going.

There were stairs that dropped below the platform I was standing on, and those stairs were one way out of the tight spot I'd gotten myself into. The problem was that the stairs didn't go all the way to the sidewalk. If I took the stairs, I'd have to jump from the last rung to the sidewalk. I couldn't tell how far it was, but from where I stood, it looked like a long way.

So I waited. And I waited. Then I had to go to the bathroom. Bad. I made a mental note to skip the two cans of root beer the next time I decided to hang out on the fire escape for an hour.

Finally I decided I had two choices. Die at the hands of my father, or die at the hands of the sidewalk below. It was a hard decision. But I decided my father might end up being a bit more forgiving than the concrete sidewalk.

I walked into the family room, and neither of them were around. I smiled and did a little skip across the floor. Maybe I could actually get to my room and throw the pan under my bed like I should have done in the first place, and everything would be fine.

I thought I just might make it when I heard my mom from her room.

"Isabel?" She peeked her head out of the bedroom. "Where have you been? You didn't leave a note."

Then she looked at the pan in my hand. "What's

that?" Now she came all the way out. "What's going on, Isabel?"

"I, um—"

Dad came out of the bathroom across from my room. "Hi, honey. We were getting a little worried. Where'd you run off to?"

"That's what I was just asking her," Mom said.

As we stood there in that cramped hallway, about a hundred lies fluttered through my brain like butterflies in a meadow. But I knew each one would result in more questions and more lies, and I'm a horrible liar.

My shoulders slumped in defeat. "These are tarts. I was trying to come up with a recipe for the baking contest. I was afraid you'd be mad that I wasn't making cupcakes, so when I heard you coming in, I ran onto the fire escape."

They both looked at me as if I had just told them I'd robbed a bank. Which right about then, sounded like a better way to make some cash than trying to make jam tarts in a cupcake house.

"I'm sorry, okay? I shouldn't have gone out there. It was stupid, I know."

"I'm disappointed in you, Isabel," said Dad. "The fire escape is off-limits. You know that."

I hung my head and nodded.

Mom took the tarts from my hand. She looked so sad, I thought she might start to cry. "You really aren't going to submit a cupcake recipe for the contest?"

I shrugged and tried to look her in the eyes, but it was too hard. I looked down at the floor again. "I, uh, I don't know. I was just playing around. You know, experimenting. I don't know what I'm going to submit yet."

Dad put his arm around Mom and took the pan of tarts with the other hand. "They look good, don't you think, Caroline? Want to try one?"

She shook her head. "No, thanks. I'm going to go lie down and read. I'm tired."

"You do that." Dad nodded. "Isabel and I are going to have a little chat about the fire escape and how it's only to be used when, you know, there's an actual *fire*."

The way he said it, I couldn't help but smile. My "thanks for trying to lighten the mood" smile.

He took her to their room while I went into the

kitchen to clean up. He came out a minute later and set the jam tarts on the counter, then walked over to me and gave me a hug.

"What am I going to do, Dad?" I said, my head resting on his chest. "Jam tarts or cupcakes?"

He pulled away and brushed my bangs out of my eyes. "I'm afraid I can't answer that for you, sweetie. It's your decision."

I sighed. He didn't have to say it with words. His eyes were begging me to make it easy on her. Easy on him. Easy on all of us.

He looked at his watch. "I gotta run. I have an appointment with a vendor downstairs. We're getting bids for the glass cases."

"Okay. See you later."

He started to walk away, then turned around. "Oh, and Is?"

"I know, Dad, I know. Stay off the fire escape. Unless there's—"

"—a fire," we both said at the same time.

"Good girl," he said as he waved and scurried out the door.

I went to my room and plopped down in my

desk chair. The thing was, jam tarts were different. Special. When I was thinking about them, and baking them, it really seemed possible that I might actually get out of Willow some day.

I took out my passport book and made a note:

A fire escape is really not
an escape at all.
Traveling to New York,
now that would be an escape.
—IB

Chapter 9

fudge brownie cupcakes

THE BEST OF BOTH WORLDS

The next couple of days were not ducky at all. I walked around like a dazed and confused cartoon character with question marks floating above my head.

Mom seemed to have her heart set on me entering a cupcake recipe. I wasn't sure it mattered, and I wondered if it would really be as great for our cupcake shop as she thought it would be.

Finally, after thinking about it so much my head actually hurt, I decided I needed to get over it and just do a cupcake recipe.

I threw myself into creating the best cupcake recipe ever. I became determined to come up with something no one had ever heard of. Nothing in the kitchen was off-limits. Boy, did I make some strange cupcakes that week.

Peppermint bubblegum cupcakes. Fruit salad cupcakes. Peanut butter, banana, and marshmallow cupcakes. The list went on and on.

I played around with recipes all week, in addition to helping Mom move all the equipment downstairs and testing a gazillion recipes for her. About then, I think I would have been over the moon with happiness if someone had told me I'd never have to eat another cupcake as long as I lived.

The shop downstairs looked better each day as we got closer and closer to the grand opening. They still needed to paint the walls inside and get the glass display cases moved in, along with a few other things. But the kitchen space in the back of the shop was ready to go. Now Mom spent most of her time down there, getting familiar with everything. After Stan raved about her cupcakes, her nerves settled down, which I felt thankful for.

Dad had taken on the role of marketing director. He was placing ads in the newspaper and on the radio, trying to get the word out about the grand opening. The telephone poles throughout town were plastered with pink and green flyers.

Things seemed to be going along pretty well, I guess. So I probably should have known something terrible would happen. I mean, isn't that how it works? Just when you think you have it made, *bam*, something bad happens.

I was on my way home from the library, the day before Sophie was due to come home, when a disaster of the worst kind happened. A disaster no one could ever have predicted. Not a natural kind of disaster. No, this disaster was of the man-made kind. A disaster called Beatrice's Brownies.

Beatrice's Brownies was the latest chain to take the nation's sweet tooth by storm. There had been stories on the news lately of cars lined up for blocks and blocks when one opened in a new location.

Part of it was the fact that the brownies had unique flavors. Bavarian cream brownies, banana split brownies, mint chocolate chip brownies, and lots more. But the other part was the experience the customer had once inside a Beatrice's Brownies store. Each customer was greeted with a brownie sample and a Dixie cup of cold milk. Then they could walk upstairs and get a firsthand view of the kitchen down below, where huge vats of brownie mix were stirred and then poured into extra-large pans. My parents and I had watched an entire TV special on the Beatrice's Brownies craze a few months back.

I about fell off my bike when I saw the sign being hoisted onto the old Burrito Shack building. They had been working on remodeling the building for a while, but not a word had been said about who or what was moving into the building. It had all been very hush-hush. But not anymore.

Cars slowed to a crawl, everyone's eyes fixed on the sign. I watched as people pointed and put their hands over their mouths. This was the biggest thing to happen to the town of Willow since the big flood of 1997, when the whole west side of town basically went under water.

I stood there, feeling sick to my stomach, like I'd eaten two dozen carrot cake cupcakes. How could we compete with Beatrice's Brownies? As the question ran through my brain over and over, only one answer kept popping up: We couldn't.

And then an even bigger question popped up. How could I tell Mom the news?

I told myself I just had to come out and tell her when I got home. But she was so happy with the strawberry lemonade cupcakes she'd made that afternoon, I couldn't do it. Then I told myself I had to tell her over dinner. Except Dad wouldn't stop talking. He told us he had passed out those strawberry lemonade cupcakes to all the workers downstairs, and they had praised her name up and down and sideways. I didn't want to be the wet blanket! Or in our case, the burnt cupcake.

Luckily, they didn't turn on the TV at all that night, so they didn't see the local news. After dinner, Mom went back down to the shop and Dad left to play cards with some teacher friends. I decided I could wait until Sophie came home to tell Mom. Sophie could help me figure out how to break the news. How to break her heart was more like it.

With the place to myself, I went into the kitchen to work on my recipe some more. The deadline was only five days away. As I pulled a bowl out of the cupboard, I thought of Mom's final list of cupcake flavors for the first month. Her list of eight looked like this:

Old-Fashioned Vanilla   Peanut Butter and Jelly
Cherry Devil's Food   Chocolate Coconut
Carrot Cake   Banana Cream Pie
Pineapple Right-Side-Up   Strawberry Lemonade

If it had been up to me, I'd have had at least one more chocolate recipe on the list. People love chocolate. Beatrice's Brownies proved that.

And that's when it hit me like a chocolate coconut cupcake upside my head. Chocolate jam tarts. Flaky, chocolaty pastry with fresh strawberry jam in the middle.

It was perfect.

Brilliant!

And absolutely, positively *not* a cupcake recipe.

Still, I wanted to try it and see how the tarts turned out. I couldn't help it. I had to know, would they taste as good as I thought they would?

I made a batch of tarts, writing the ingredients down on a recipe card as I went along.

They tasted *so* good! In a word, amazing.

I paced the kitchen floor as I finished the tart, my thoughts and feelings chasing each other round and round, like a puppy chasing his tail.

After a good thirty minutes, I figured out, it really came down to one question: Make myself happy or make my mother happy?

I had to choose. Simple as that.

Except there wasn't anything even close to simple about it.

Chapter 10

s'mores cupcakes
CAN'T GO WRONG WITH CHOCOLATY
MARSHMALLOW PERFECTION

I thought about calling Grandma and asking her for advice. But I'd already asked her that day when I first told her and Mom about the contest. She'd told me to follow my heart. She'd said I had a good heart. A good heart?

A girl with a good heart would set her own feelings aside, I thought. That was the good thing to do. The right thing to do. Even if it was the sad thing to do. Sad to me, anyway. Submitting a cupcake recipe would make Mom happy. I needed to do it for her.

With that, I made up my mind. For good this time. I dumped the rest of the tarts into the garbage can, hoping I hadn't just dumped my chances to go to New York City right along with them.

Then I got back to work, wishing and hoping I could come up with a fantastically amazing cupcake recipe. I still had chocolate on the brain, and I was thinking about Sophie coming home the next day and wondering what recipe she would make, when I remembered talking about s'mores. Chocolaty marshmallow perfection, Sophie had called them. Well, what if I put that chocolaty marshmallow perfection into a cupcake?

I stayed up into the wee hours of the morning mixing and baking, perfecting the recipe. When Mom came in late herself, I had her taste the latest batch. She smiled and said it was delicious. Then she said good night and headed to her room. I'll admit I had hoped for a bit more encouragement. More excitement. More something. But she was tired, and

I told myself it didn't matter, I had a recipe to enter (even if it wasn't the best chocolate jam tart recipe ever to be invented).

When I went to my room, I wrote the cupcake recipe on a card in my best handwriting, put it in an envelope, and stuck it in my desk drawer until I could get the mailing address from Sophie. Then I wrote in my passport book:

> *Maybe someday*
> *I can live somewhere in England*
> *and open a jam tart shop.*
> *I wonder, would I long*
> *to visit Willow then?*
> *—IB*

I fell into bed that night exhausted and slept late, which wasn't like me. Usually the morning traffic on the road in front of our building woke me, but I slept through it.

When I finally did wake up, my first thought was that Sophie would be home soon. The happiness in that thought was quickly replaced with a sickening sadness when I had my second thought. I needed to tell Mom about Beatrice's Brownies.

After I threw on my robe, I went to my window, slid it open, and put my cheek against the screen. The blue sky and warm air told me it was going to be hot. Down below, two ladies stood at the corner, one of them pointing at the cupcake sign. They walked up to the building and peeked inside the window.

I knew Mom, without the gumption gene, wouldn't take the news about Beatrice's well. But I also believed, as I watched those ladies, our cupcake shop could be something special. I just needed to figure out how to convince my mother of that.

I found Dad sitting at the kitchen table, his hands hugging a cup of coffee and the Sunday paper laid out in front of him. On the front page it read WILLOW WELCOMES BEATRICE'S BROWNIES and below it was a big picture of the sign I'd seen yesterday.

"Dad?" I asked.

He jumped a little, startled to hear my voice.

"Hey, good morning, punkin."

I pointed at the paper. "Did Mom see that?"

He shook his head. "She's in the bathroom. We

need to tell her when she comes out. It's important that she hear it from us."

I sat down. "I saw them putting the sign up yesterday, on my way home from the library. I should have told her last night. But I just couldn't."

He nodded. "I know. It's hard." He took a drink of coffee. "At least it doesn't open until Labor Day weekend. That buys us some time. I mean, hopefully she'll see it's not the end of the world. We're just going to have to work a little harder, that's all."

I gave him a funny look. Was he talking about my mother?

We sat there, waiting. "You hungry?" he asked me.

I shook my head. Then the phone rang.

I jumped up and grabbed the phone in the kitchen.

"Hello?"

"Isabel, it's Grandma. Did you hear the news?"

I sighed. "Yeah. Dad and I are here, waiting to tell Mom."

"Tell me what?" I heard Mom's voice from behind me.

"I'll be right over," Grandma said.

"Okay. Bye, Grandma."

I hung up and walked back over to the table.

I looked at Dad. He looked at me. I think about then we were both wishing for a miracle. Like suddenly the president of the United States would declare brownies unfit to eat and brownie shops everywhere would be forced to close. Or a big rock band would swing through town, see our shop, and write a song about it. It'd shoot to number one and our shop would be famous. They'd put me in their music video. And insist I come on tour with them. And . . .

"Tell me what, Isabel?" Mom said again.

Dad walked over and put his arm around Mom. "Honey, I don't know how to say this, so I'm just going to come right out with it. Beatrice's Brownies is opening a store near here. It made the front page of the newspaper today."

I watched as her cherry-pink cheeks turned the color of buttercream.

"Mom, it's really not that big of a deal. I mean, okay, yeah, it's Beatrice's Brownies. But the excitement will wear off, and people will realize that a cute cupcake shop is way better than a stupid chain brownie store."

Her shoulders slumped, and one hand reached up to her heart, as if her hand pressed there could keep it from beating too fast. "Beatrice's Brownies? Here in Willow?"

Both Dad and I nodded. He handed her the newspaper. "It's going to be all right, though, Caroline. I was telling Isabel, we just have to work a little harder."

She stared at the picture in the paper. "Work a little harder? Are you kidding? We could work day and night for months and never come close to getting the kind of business they're going to get. And once you have a box of scrumptious brownies, you think you're going to stop and get a box of cupcakes, too? Of course you're not. Which means we're doomed. Doomed before we even had a chance." She threw the paper on the table and stomped down the hall to her room.

After her door shut, I asked Dad, "What do we do now?"

He got up and grabbed his clipboard off the

kitchen counter. "I don't know. I'll be back later. I need some air."

As he walked toward the door, I wanted to tell him to go in there and be a cheerleader. He was giving up too easily. He needed to give her his best rah-rah-rah! But my dad's not like that. He's never been like that. Give him a fraction to reduce or a project to work on, and he's all over it. But words of encouragement? Not his thing. I thought about making him a list.

1. Use a soft, calm voice.
2. Smile, but not too much, or it looks fake.
3. General phrases like "Try not to worry" or "It'll be okay" are good.
4. And specific words that will make her smile and feel good about herself and her cupcakes are even better. What those specific words might be, I don't know, since I'm not good at that kind of thing.

I started to get up and go in there myself, and try to find the right words. But something told me she wouldn't listen to me. Because I'd had my doubts. I had told her a Laundromat would be better than a cupcake shop. Easier than a cupcake shop. And knowing her, she'd probably remind me of that.

I sat there, staring at the picture on the front page, wishing it would disappear, so maybe, just once, Mom could be happy. And maybe, just once, all of us could be happy.

Right then, it seemed about as impossible as me flying across the world and seeing the Great Wall of China.

Chapter 11

hawaiian sky cupcakes

THE BLUE COCONUT BUTTERCREAM

WILL MAKE YOU GO WOW

Grandma came over, all dressed up in an emerald green dress along with little white gloves and a white hat with a feather. She marched down the hall and told Mom she had five minutes to get ready because they were going out.

"I think the best thing to do today is get her out of here and get her mind off cupcakes for a while. Let her stew for too long, and she'll be ready to give up for sure. Wouldn't you agree, Izzy?"

I nodded. Grandma always seemed to have the right answer.

"Do you want to go with us, honey?"

"Sophie's coming home today. She's been gone three whole weeks. I can't wait to see her. Is that all right?"

"Of course. I know this is hard for you, too. You should go see your friend and have a ducky good time. Tomorrow we'll regroup. Make a plan. And we must never, never, never give in. That's what Winston Churchill said, Isabel. He was a wise man. We would do well to follow his advice. Your grandpa met one of his relatives, you know. I can't quite remember her name. But, oh, your grandfather was tickled pink about meeting one of Churchill's relatives, that's for sure."

"Never give in," I said. "Okay. I'll try."

She shook her finger at me and smiled. "Never, never, *never* give in. That's three nevers. Got it?"

"Got it."

She hugged me. "It'll be okay, my darlin' Izzy. You'll see."

The phone rang, so I ran to get it, hoping it was Sophie.

"Chickarita!" she shouted in my ear. "I'm home!"

I squealed. "Yay! Can I come over?"

"Yeah. Just be prepared. Suitcases and dirty clothes are everywhere! They might put you to work doing laundry or something. On second thought, I'll wait for you out front. Hurry, before they suck me into the bottomless pit of chores to be done."

I laughed. "Okay. I'll be right there. I have so much to tell you!"

"Oh, good. Hey, wanna go to the Blue Moon? I'm craving some fries big-time. Plus, that way, Hayden can't barge in and interrupt us with stories of how aliens are here on earth, living among us, ready to snatch us at any given moment and take us back to their planet for research."

"I'm on my way. Bye."

After I hung up, Grandma said, "I presume she's home?"

"Yep. I'm going over there and we're going out to lunch. Tell Mom where I'm at?"

She nodded. "I'll be sure to tell her. And I'll leave your dad a note. Have fun!"

I flew out the door and down the stairs, then grabbed my bike from the storage closet underneath the stairs.

Just then, a pretty woman in shorts and a T-shirt with long black hair walked up to the door, carrying a suitcase and wheeling one case behind her.

I quickly put the kickstand down and went and opened the door for her.

"Thanks," she said, walking in and dropping everything in front of her. "You must be one of the new neighbors." She stuck her hand out. "I'm Lana. I live in the third apartment upstairs."

I took her hand and shook it. Gently but firmly, like my grandpa had taught me when I was three years old. "Oh, hi. I'm Isabel. I wondered when you'd be back. Stan said you were on a trip?"

She nodded. "I'm just getting back from staying with my family in Hawaii. That's where I'm originally from."

"Oh, cool," I said. "Which island?"

"The Big Island."

"Wow. I'd love to go there someday." I pointed to her suitcases. "Want some help carrying these upstairs?"

"Oh, that'd be great. Thanks. Times like this it'd be nice to have an elevator, you know?"

I grabbed one of the suitcases and started up the stairs. "Is Hawaii as beautiful as it looks in pictures?"

I could hear her flip-flops clicking behind me. "Well, even more so, I think. No other place like it, really."

When we reached the top of the stairs, I stopped and let her go ahead of me. She pulled her keys out of her purse.

"Is it your family who is opening the cupcake shop?" she asked.

"Hopefully. I mean, we're supposed to open August fifteenth."

She turned back and looked at me, a puzzled look on her face. "You don't sound too sure. Things not going well?"

"Oh, they're going fine, I guess. We're just nervous

because Beatrice's Brownies is going to be opening a few blocks over."

She fiddled with her keys, trying to find the right one. "Well, I like cupcakes a lot better than brownies, so you'll have at least one customer. I'll have to mark my calendar."

The door swung open, and she hung back so I could go in ahead of her. Past the little entryway was the family room, just like our apartment. But that was where the similarities ended.

"Whoa," I said as I set the suitcase down. Every wall was painted with a beautiful Hawaiian scene. Palm trees, a blue and green ocean, surfers, and even a girl doing the hula in a grass skirt.

"This is incredible. Who did it?" I asked, looking at Lana.

She smiled. "I did. I'm so glad you like it."

"You're an artist? Really? Do you do paintings, too, or just, um, walls?"

She laughed. "Murals are my specialty, but yes, I also paint on canvas."

Just then, I realized that Sophie would probably

be wondering about me. "Oh, man, I have to go. Sorry, Lana. My friend is waiting for me."

"No problem. It was great meeting you, Isabel. I'll go over and introduce myself to your parents. I'm sure I'll see you around."

"Bye!"

I ran down the stairs and hopped on my bike, my feet pumping faster than the thoughts whirling around in my brain. Now I had one more cool thing to tell Sophie. So much had happened in the past few weeks, I didn't even know where to start.

A few minutes later I reached the street with the yellow duplex that I'd called home for five fun-filled years. When Sophie saw me pedaling toward her, she jumped out of the grass where she'd been sitting and came running down the sidewalk, waving her arms in the air like a crazy person.

Laughing, I glided to a stop and put my foot down. I stood beneath a tall maple tree in front of a big white Colonial-style house Mom had always admired. It was hot out, and I'd worked up a sweat on the short ride over. It felt nice to stand in the cool shade for a couple of seconds, the smell of cut grass drifting through the air.

Once Sophie reached me, she grabbed my hand, jumping up and down, flapping my arm as she screamed, "I'm home, I'm home, I'm home!"

I laughed. "I know, I know, I know!"

"Did you miss me?" she asked.

"Are you kidding? I have so much to tell you. Get your bike and let's get something to eat!"

While I waited for her, I pulled out my passport book for a quick note, since Lana's and Sophie's trips were both on my mind.

> *There are so many places I want to visit.*
> *When I'm a flight attendant,*
> *I can visit the Grand Canyon one day*
> *and be in Hawaii the next.*
> *I can't imagine*
> *a more perfect job.*
> *—IB*

We couldn't really talk while we rode, because we had to ride single file in the bike lane. When we finally got to the Blue Moon, we both started talking as we walked up to the door.

"Okay, just hold on," Sophie said with a giggle. "We have to be orderly about this. You know, like show-and-tell in first grade. First I'll share something and you listen. Then you share something and I'll listen."

"Hey," I said, crossing my arms and sticking my bottom lip out. "No fair. You get to go first."

She laughed and pulled me inside the diner, a wave of cool air greeting us. A waitress walked by, carrying two plates with burgers and fries. The smell made my stomach rumble. "Go ahead and sit anywhere, girls," the waitress said. "I'll get you some water right away."

The Blue Moon is this funky little retro place where a lot of the middle school and high school kids like to hang out. Black-and-white pictures of our town back in the fifties and sixties hang on the walls. There's a jukebox in the corner, and the booths are the old style with red vinyl seats.

As the Beatles song "Yellow Submarine" blared from the jukebox, we slid into a booth, the waitress right behind us with two glasses of water and menus. "Hot out there?" she asked.

We both nodded as we picked up the glasses and started chugging.

"I'll be back to take your order," she said.

My lips tingled from the cold water. I set my glass down. "Okay. Start."

She stuck her finger in the air as she finished draining her glass.

"Sophie, how dare you quench your thirst at a time like this. Talk. Now!"

She started laughing, which meant water spewed out of her mouth and all over the table.

Then *I* was laughing. I grabbed some napkins from the silver napkin dispenser and wiped up the mess.

"Ah," she said, once she got her laughter under control, "I missed you, Chickarita."

"I missed you, too, Sophie Bird. Now start."

"Okay, first, remember I wrote in my letter to you that camp was not fun? You got my letter, right?" I nodded. "Good. Well, the day after I mailed that, guess what?"

"What?" I asked.

"It got fun. I mean, really fun." She leaned in like she had to tell me the world's best secret. "Fun you spell like this: K-Y-L-E."

Chapter 12

pink champagne cupcakes

SWEET YET SOPHISTICATED,

JUST LIKE GRANDMA

My mouth flew open. "You met a boy?"

She nodded. "He's so cute. And funny. Hilariously funny. You would like him. He's just like us."

"How old is he? Where does he live? Are you, like, boyfriend and girlfriend now?"

"Whoa, wait a sec. Okay, let's see. He's going into

eighth grade, so one year older than me. He lives in a small town in Washington. It's close enough so we *could* visit each other. Maybe. And my boyfriend? How am I supposed to know? We held hands three times and we hugged twice. Oh, and we wrote each other lots of notes. So what do you think? Boyfriend and girlfriend?"

"Sounds like you are to me!"

She clapped her hands together and squealed. "Oh, good, I think so too." But then the corners of her mouth turned down, and the sparkle from her eyes disappeared. "Still, I can't stand it that I don't even know when I'll see him again."

I nodded, like I'd had ten boyfriends and I understood, even though I hadn't had one and I really didn't.

The waitress came back, and we ordered two shakes along with an order of fries to share.

"Okay, your turn," she said.

"Mine comes in three parts. First part. I got fired from my babysitting job at Mrs. Canova's."

Her mouth dropped open. "No way. Are you serious?"

"I left them alone in the backyard for about a

millisecond, and she freaked out. Okay, so there was a pool of water involved and she had every right to be furious, but still. Firing me was kind of extreme, wasn't it?"

She nodded. "Very."

"Second part. My recipe's all ready to go for the contest. I just need the address."

"Holy guacamole, I have to get cooking," she said. "Literally."

"Yeah, Soph, you better. August first is just a few days away."

She leaned back in her seat, tucking her hair behind her ears. "No problem. I'll whip something up tonight or tomorrow, and get it in the mail. Remind me to give you the address when I get home. Okay, what's the third part?"

"The third part is the worst." She leaned in when I said that, her eyes big and round. "Beatrice's Brownies is going to open just a few blocks away from us. Mom is devastated. Like so devastated, I think she wants to give up."

"No!" Sophie said. "She can't give up. You guys have worked so hard."

The waitress brought our fries and milk shakes. We started sipping on our shakes, both of us quiet for a minute.

"We have to figure out a way to help her," Sophie said. "I know we can make the cupcake shop work. I just know it."

"You'd better come over a lot in the next couple of weeks," I told her as I took the ketchup bottle and squirted some on the french fry plate. "You need to rub some of that determination onto my mother."

The next morning I got out the contest address Sophie had given me the day before and wrote it down on the envelope that held my recipe. I found a stamp in the desk in the family room, walked down to the corner and, with my fingers crossed, dropped the envelope into the big blue mailbox.

The magazine didn't say when finalists would be contacted, but I guessed it would be awhile. I wanted to be selected more than anything I'd ever wanted, but it was out of my hands now. I had other things to worry about, anyway.

The construction workers were back in full

force. A truck sat out front, and guys were carrying enormous boxes from the truck into the shop. I figured the glass cases had finally arrived. The cases where the cupcakes would be beautifully displayed, causing little kids to lean onto the glass, oohing and aahing, their grimy fingerprints a gift they'd leave behind for me to wipe away with a bottle of Windex and a good rag.

"Good morning," Grandma's voice said from behind me.

I turned around. Today she wore a navy blue skirt with a pale yellow jacket and a big floppy navy blue hat.

"Grandma," I said, "you're here early."

"We need to have a family meeting. You know, get our cupcakes in a row. Your mother and I didn't discuss business at all yesterday. She loosened up a couple of hours into our shopping trip, and I think she had a good time. But now it's back to work."

I nodded. "Grandma, we're so lucky to have you. What would we do without you?"

She looped her arm through mine, and we went inside. "Well, Izzy, I'm glad I have you, too."

Upstairs, Mom made pancakes while Dad read the newspaper.

"Grandma's here," I called out as we walked in.

We sat at the table, and Mom brought a plate of steaming pancakes over along with a small pitcher of warm syrup. "Would you like a plate, Mom?" she asked.

"No, thank you. I've already eaten. I'll take some coffee, though, if you have it."

Dad and I started piling pancakes on our plates, while Mom poured Grandma her cup of coffee.

"This week," Grandma said, looking very businesslike, "we all need to focus on advertising. Every minute of every day needs to be getting the word out about the cupcake shop. I ordered some postcards with coupons we can send out. We definitely need to get around town and pass out samples. Oh, and I've contacted a newspaper reporter who would like to interview us."

"A newspaper reporter?" Dad asked as he wiped his mouth with a napkin. "That's great, Dolores. How'd you manage that?"

"Easy," she said, as Mom slipped a mug of steaming

coffee in front of Grandma, then sat down beside me. "I called the paper up and told them they were missing out on the truly interesting stories surrounding the opening of Beatrice's Brownies. How is a big, corporate, national chain going to affect family businesses? Is it the kiss of death? Will one small business be finished before it ever even started?"

"Mother!" Mom gasped. "We have to talk about ourselves in comparison to Beatrice's? I don't want to do that. Why can't we just talk about It's Raining Cupcakes? You know, what we have to offer and why we're special?"

"Because," said Dad, "your mother is a genius. A story like this will garner sympathy. It will get people in our corner. It's exactly what we need. Nice job, Dolores."

My mom sighed. "Are you sure this is a good idea?"

Grandma nodded. "Completely ducky. Beatrice's Brownies will be the villain. We'll come out smelling like roses. Or cupcakes, in this instance."

I smiled as I finished the last bite of pancake. I was right. We were *really* lucky to have Grandma.

"So when's the interview?" Dad asked.

Grandma tapped her watch. "Today. One o'clock."

"Today?" cried Mom. "No, no, no. I can't do it today. That's too soon."

Grandma reached over, put her hand on Mom's arm, and spoke in her calm but firm voice. "It's not too soon, Caroline. It's just in time. We need to get the word out about the shop now. And honestly, I don't want to give you a whole lot of time to fret over it. We'll do it today, and it'll be over with."

Mom stood up and paced the floor. "I just don't know. I don't know if I can do it. David, can he interview you? I'm not good at this kind of thing."

"How about if he interviews all of us?" I suggested. "He can ask a question and whoever wants to answer it does."

"Sure," Grandma said. "I think that's a fine way to handle it. After all, every one of us is invested in this thing one way or another. Not just Caroline."

I looked at the clock in the kitchen. It said 10:10. "We have three hours to clean the place up and get ready. What should I wear, Grandma?"

She smiled. "It's all taken care of. Your mother and I bought you some new clothes yesterday on our shopping expedition. Wait until you see what I picked out for you!"

I stood in my bedroom, looking in the full-length mirror hung on the back of my door. How do you spell style? G-R-A-N-D-M-A! Boy, did she know how to pick it out.

She'd bought me a cute pink sundress with a black, short-sleeved jacket trimmed in pink that went over it. I hardly ever wore dresses, but this one made me want to wear them more often. She'd also bought me a pair of black sandals with short heels (which I now wore), two pairs of pants, and some fun summer tops to go with them.

I heard the doorbell ring and looked at my watch. It wasn't quite one o'clock, so I assumed it was Sophie. She'd called while I was dusting earlier, and when I told her we were getting ready to meet with a newspaper reporter, she'd asked if she could come and watch.

I heard Grandma's heels *tap*, *tap*, *tap* across the

hardwood floor. I decided to let her greet Sophie and send her back to my room so I could surprise her with my newfound style.

When she opened my door, she gasped and cried, "Whoa, Chickarita!"

I spun around. "You like?"

"But you're not done yet," she said, as if she was talking about a tray of cupcakes baking in the oven. "We need to do something about your hair. Come. Sit down."

She nudged me over to the chair in front of my desk and grabbed my hairbrush off the dresser. "Do you have any barrettes or ribbons or anything?"

This coming from the girl with the best hair in town. Natural blond, wavy—but not in an obnoxious frizzy way—and totally cooperative with whatever she wants to do with it on any given day.

"Sophie, my hair is short. I don't need barrettes, and I never put anything in my hair. You know that."

"You don't have *anything*?" she asked.

I shook my head.

"Hold on. Let me go see if you have something I can work with."

She walked out and left me sitting there, wondering what was so wrong with my hair. It was brown, it was short, and I never had to do anything to it. Just wash it and go. Then I realized, maybe *that's* what was wrong with it. Maybe it looked like all I did was wash it and go.

She came back with a bottle of gel Mom had gotten ages ago at the salon. I think she used it one time and never touched it again.

"Sophie? What are you going to do exactly?"

She squirted some of the gel into her hands and rubbed them together. "I don't know. I just want to try something."

I sat there as she rubbed the stuff through my hair, trying to sculpt it this way, then that way. She worked a lot on my bangs, trying to force them over to one side. She was taking forever. Then the doorbell rang.

"He's here!" I yelled, jumping up and whacking her in the chin in the process.

"Ow!" she cried.

"Sorry. Come on. We have to go."

I turned and faced her.

"Oh no," she said.

"What? What's wrong?"

I dashed over to the mirror. And shrieked. "Sophie! I look like Elvis. Only uglier!"

She tried to laugh. "I guess a little of that gel goes a long way. But come on, it doesn't look *too* bad."

"Doesn't look too bad? Are you kidding me?"

I grabbed the brush, bent over so my hair hung upside down, and brushed my hair as hard as I could. I thought maybe I could brush some of the gel out and fluff my hair a little bit. But when I flipped my head back and stood up, my hair stuck straight up everywhere.

Sophie burst out laughing.

"Girls, come on, the reporter's here," I heard Grandma say.

I peeked out of my bedroom. Grandma was looking right at me, and she clapped her hand to her mouth.

"I need another minute, Grandma." She nodded, her eyes wide with both shock and amusement.

I shut the door again and started brushing, my best friend laughing so hard she was absolutely no help. Not that I wanted her help, of course. I decided I never wanted her help again.

At least when it came to my hair.

Chapter 13

cherry devil's food cupcakes

WHEN YOU NEED SOMETHING DEVILISH TO MATCH YOUR MOOD

When Sophie finally stopped rolling around on my bed and wiping tears from her eyes, the first words out of her mouth were, "Put on a hat!"

"A hat?" I cried. "Okay, if it were the middle of February, maybe a stocking hat and some gloves would work. But it's summer, ya loonhead."

She started to laugh again. "Not a stocking hat. You know, a fancy hat, like your grandma wears. Don't you have any old hats she's given you?"

It seemed like the only solution. I ran to my closet and started digging through the piles of old clothes I'd set aside to be taken to Goodwill. Underneath the pile, I found a funny-looking black hat with a little piece of netting that hung in front. Right. Perfect if we were going to a funeral.

"Isabel!" my dad called. "Hurry up. We're waiting for you!"

I tossed aside a blue one with a big white flower on the side. Ug-lee! And then, from way in the back of my closet, I pulled out a little pink hat with a bow along the side.

I dusted it off and fluffed it up, then stuck it on and ran to the mirror. It wasn't bad. "What do you think?" I asked.

"Just ducky. Now go out there and sell cupcakes!"

I walked out like I'd been planning to wear the hat all along. Grandma gave me the biggest grin when she saw me.

"Like grandmother, like granddaughter," Dad said to Mom.

"Hi, Isabel," the reporter said, sticking his hand out. "I'm Patrick."

"Very pleased to meet you," I said, trying to sound as sophisticated as Grandma when she says it.

The four of us sat on the couch, while Patrick sat across from us in the La-Z-Boy. Since there weren't any more seats, Sophie stood next to the end of the couch.

Patrick started off by asking Mom and Dad questions about the original concept of a cupcake shop, who came up with it, why did they think it would be successful, that kind of thing. Then he got into asking us how we felt about Beatrice's Brownies.

"Well," Grandma said, "I'm sure you can understand our lack of enthusiasm over the opening of the store. They are a huge corporation and have mostly targeted large cities. Until now. Why come here, to our cozy town of Willow? What is there for them to gain? Not a thing, except crushing the hopes and dreams of families just like ours, who are trying to make a decent living in the neighborhoods where we grew up."

"What do you think, Isabel?" Patrick asked me. "Have you ever had a brownie from Beatrice's? Think the kids will prefer them over your cupcakes?"

I put my hand on my stomach, the butterflies flapping their wings hard in there. He'd asked me a question directly. I had to answer him.

I smoothed my dress across my lap and started talking. "No, I've never had one of their brownies. But we watched a special about them on TV. Their brownies look pretty good, I guess. And people seem to like them. Will kids want brownies or cupcakes? Well, I hope they'll want cupcakes, but we'll just have to wait and see."

I sat back and breathed a sigh of relief that it was over. I'd been as honest as I could be. I glanced over at Sophie, expecting to see a thumbs-up. Instead her eyes were bugging out of her head; she was waving her hands back and forth and mouthing the words, *No, no, NO!*

Dad noticed and spoke up. "Sophie, is there something you'd like to say? We've known you for so long, you're like part of the family now. Come over here and take a seat."

He got up and made room for Sophie to sit next to Mom. Patrick asked Sophie for her full name and wrote it down in the little notebook he'd brought with him.

"What about you, Sophie? Think the folks in Willow will prefer brownies over cupcakes?"

"Are you kidding me?" said Sophie. "No way. Those brownies are terrible. They aren't chock-full of chocolaty goodness like the commercials say. More like chock-full of artificial flavors and preservatives. We can guarantee you that It's Raining Cupcakes will give you a fresh, homemade cupcake just like Grandma used to make every single time you come to visit."

And with that, she pointed to Grandma and smiled, like the reporter had a TV camera in his hand instead of a notebook.

I sat there fuming, my hands balled up into tight fists. The nerve! How could she make my answer sound completely wrong? It wasn't wrong. It was honest. Besides, how did she even know the brownies were terrible? Had she ever tried one? What if the company sued her for saying something mean like that?

I started to speak, to add something more newsworthy to my answer, when Sophie piped in with some more words of wonderful wisdom.

"I'm so sure people like cupcakes better than brownies, or any other dessert for that matter, I entered a cupcake recipe in a special baking contest for kids. Just you wait. I bet my cupcake recipe will win!"

I couldn't believe it. Out of all the desserts she could have entered, she'd picked a cupcake recipe? I glared at her and almost said something, but just then the doorbell rang.

Patrick jumped up from his chair. "That'll be the photographer. I want to get a picture of all of you downstairs, in front of the shop. Then I'll have a few more questions for David and Caroline, if that's okay."

They nodded, and we all stood up. When Sophie finally looked at me, she gave me the thumbs-up sign. By then I was sure she was out to make me look as stupid as possible. First the hair and then making me look bad during the interview. What was next? Pushing me out of the photo at the last second?

Dad greeted the photographer, and then we all walked downstairs. Sophie walked beside my grandma, chatting it up with her like they were best friends.

I reached up and fixed my silly hat, knowing I needed to stand next to Grandma for the photo, so people would think we dressed up like that on purpose. As I walked down the stairs, I saw Lana getting her mail.

"Hey, Lana," I yelled, waving at her.

"Hi, Isabel," she called back.

Sophie looked back at me, a question mark in her eyes. I had forgotten to tell her about Lana and her beautiful murals. Well, good. Let her wonder who the strange, pretty lady was who knew my name.

Outside, the photographer arranged us the way he wanted. The three adults stood in back, and Sophie and I stood in front of them. "I need to switch with her," I told him.

"How come?" Sophie asked.

"So the only two ladies wearing hats in the photo are standing next to each other."

"It doesn't matter," said Sophie.

"Well it matters—," I didn't get to finish.

"Fine," the photographer said. "Doesn't make

any difference to me. Please switch and let's get this going while the sun is behind a cloud. Makes for a much better picture that way."

We made the switch, and then he said, "Say 'cupcakes.'" I didn't say "cupcakes" and I didn't smile, since I couldn't find one single thing to smile about.

Patrick pulled Mom and Dad aside to talk to them a little more. Sophie and I stood there on the sidewalk with Grandma.

"I think it went just ducky, don't you, girls?"

I didn't answer. I was too mad. But Sophie spouted off a bunch of stuff, including how she was positive no one would eat at Beatrice's once they read the article and learned that Beatrice's brownies were filled with artificial flavors and preservatives.

It was then that I found my voice. My loud voice. "Sophie, do you even know if that's *true*? I don't think you should have said that. There are better ways to earn customers, don't you think?"

Her mouth dropped open, like she couldn't believe what she'd just heard. I wanted to pop a cupcake into her big mouth. A whole carrot cake cupcake. Unfrosted.

"Well it was better than what you said, Miss Wishy-Washy. 'I hope they'll want cupcakes, but we'll just have to wait and see.' I thought the whole reason for the article was to MAKE PEOPLE WANT TO EAT YOUR CUPCAKES!"

"Okay, girls," Grandma said, "that's enough. Come on. You both had the best of intentions. And you did a lovely job. Now patch things up between you, what do you say?"

Neither of us said anything for what seemed like forever.

"Sorry, Isabel," Sophie finally said. "I was just trying to help. But I'm going home now. You're obviously mad at me. Call me later if you want."

Before I could say anything, she took off down the sidewalk and around the corner.

Grandma pulled me to her and gave me a hug. "For goodness' sake, Isabel, what is wrong? One minute everything's ducky, and the next it's like World War Three."

I looked down and kicked a little pebble across the sidewalk. "I can't stand it, Grandma. She does everything better than me. And what she wants, she gets. It's not fair. She has a dog, and she even got to see the Grand Canyon, a boyfriend,

Grandma laughed. "I didn't even know you want a dog. Or a boyfriend."

I leaned up against the front window of the cupcake shop, the glass cool on my back. "I don't. But I guess she did. And she got what she wanted. That's my point. I want to go on a trip. Do I get to go? No. I want Mom to be happy. Is she? Mostly no! I want to look good for a picture in the paper, and something as simple as that doesn't even work out. See what I mean? I don't even know why I entered that stupid baking contest. Of course she's going to win."

"But you entered?" Grandma asked.

"Yes. I mailed it yesterday."

She reached out and grabbed my hand, then gently rubbed it with hers. It felt small against mine. Fragile. "Things don't always go our way, Izzy. But I'm proud of you for sticking your neck out and trying. If you don't try, nothing happens. But if you try, well, you just never know. That's what you want your mom to understand, right?"

sighed. "I miss the old days, Anna. I miss the days when Mom and I would bake together because it was fun. Will it ever be fun again?"

"I do believe it will be," she said, pulling on my hand, leading me back to the door to go inside. "Think positively. Stay focused on the possibilities. What do you say?"

I couldn't answer. Because I was starting to believe less and less in possibilities and more and more in plain, rotten luck.

Chapter 14

old-fashioned
vanilla cupcakes

FOR THOSE WHO LOVE THE FAMILIAR

J didn't call Sophie. And she didn't call me. Instead I threw myself into the cupcake business. Grandma and I made about a gazillion cupcakes over the next week and went around the whole town, passing them out to anyone and everyone. We stood in front of the library, the swimming pool, and Mother Goose Park. Along with the cupcakes, we gave people a postcard Grandma had made with a coupon for two dollars off the purchase of a dozen cupcakes. Again and again, people told us how delicious the cupcakes were and that they'd be sure to stop in when the shop opened.

Of course, Mom didn't hear any of it because she stayed home. She mostly sat in her room, or on the couch watching TV. We tried everything to get her to come with us, but she seemed determined to give up.

I went to the library and checked out a bunch of books to see if something might help her. Some of them had pretty interesting titles.

Don't Be a Fraidy Cat: How to Live Like You Have Nine Lives
How to Find Your Happy Place in a Sad World
From Worrywart to Hopeful Hero in Ten Easy Steps

I left a couple on the coffee table in the family room and a few others on the nightstand in her room, so all she had to do was pick one up and start reading.

"We only have another week until we open," I

said to Dad one night while he and I sat watching TV. "What if she can't do it? Are *you* going to bake cupcakes?"

He turned and gave me a slight smile. "I'm a fine cupcake baker, thank you very much."

"Fine cupcake eater is more like it," I said.

"That too," he said, standing up. "And now I'm going to bed. Don't stay up too late."

"Good night, Dad."

"Good night, sweetheart."

"Hey, Dad?" I said, before he reached the hallway.

He stopped and turned to me. "Yes?"

"Do you think everything's going to be okay?"

He put his hand up and rubbed his scruffy cheek. "Yes, I do. We just have to carry Mom through this right now. She doesn't believe, so we'll believe for her until she's ready. That's what families do, you know?"

"Yeah."

He turned around. "See you in the morning."

Suddenly I felt tired. Exhausted. I thought about what Dad said as I turned off the TV and went to my room. In my passport book, I wrote:

When I travel, I will pay someone
to carry my luggage everywhere I go.
It will just be so much easier that way.

—IB

The next morning Dad woke me up, shaking me and saying my name.

I sat up, afraid the place was on fire or something. "What is it? What?"

"Look!" he said. "They put us on the front page!"

He shoved the paper in my face. I had to blink a few times to focus.

The headline read, LOCAL FAMILY KEEN ON CUPCAKES, NOT BROWNIES.

When I saw the picture, I wanted to throw up. I looked completely ridiculous in the hat. On Grandma a hat looked normal. Stylish. But on a twelve-year-old girl? Just. Plain. Stupid.

I fell back and pulled the covers over my head.

"What?" Dad said. "What's wrong?"

"Nothing," I mumbled. "I need to wake up. I'll be out in a little while. I'll read the article then."

He got up and left me alone to consider my options.

A. Use my babysitting money to buy up every newspaper I could get my hands on and then burn them.

B. Hitch a ride to Idaho and take up residency there.

C. Color my hair purple so no one would recognize me as the girl in the stupid hat.

D. Just accept the fact that I was the stupid girl in the hat, and it would blow over eventually.

I got up and put my robe on. At least Dad seemed happy about the article. Then I remembered what Sophie had said during the interview, and I wanted to see if they'd put it in the article.

I walked out and grabbed the paper off the table.

"Has Mom seen it yet?" I asked.

"No. She's still asleep. I hope it cheers her up."

I scanned the article, looking for quotes. My name

was mentioned only once, in the beginning, when we were introduced as the family who owned the shop. Nothing I actually said was included. Sophie, on the other hand—"a close family friend," according to the article—was quoted as saying, "It's Raining Cupcakes will give you a fresh, homemade cupcake just like Grandma used to make."

Even though Sophie sounded like she was being paid to plug our cupcakes, it was a good article. The reporter wrote about the different flavors, the flavor-of-the-month idea, and the hominess of the shop. I could see people reading it and wanting to come and try our cupcakes.

"Well?" Dad asked.

"It's good. Really good. Except for the picture, where I look totally ridiculous. But it should make Mom feel better."

He stood there, sipping his coffee. "I think it's good too. Maybe her fear will lessen a bit after she reads it."

"What are we doing today?" I asked. "Passing out more cupcakes?"

Dad shook his head. "We're taking the day off. You

deserve it. Why don't you and Soph go to the pool? Or see a movie? Get out and have some fun."

"I don't know. I'm pretty tired. Maybe I'll just stick around here. Read a book or something."

"Whatever you want," he said, heading toward the bathroom. "I'm going to get ready for the day."

I sat down at the table and flipped the paper over, so I wouldn't have to look at the embarrassing photo. I imagined Sophie looking at it and dropping to the floor in hysterics. She'd probably cut it out and send it to her *boyfriend.* They'd write back and forth about the idiotic girl wearing the old-lady hat. Sophie would brag about how she was totally going to beat the idiotic girl in the baking contest she'd entered. He'd tell her that of course she would beat the idiotic girl. She was good at everything. Not just good. Fantastic.

Mom came out of her room, snapping me out of my depressing thoughts. She walked over to the coffeepot and poured herself a cup without a word. It was like I wasn't even there.

"Mom? The article ran today. You know, the article on the cupcake shop? It's really good." I got up and tried to hand her the newspaper.

She swatted at it and turned her head away. "I don't want to read it. It doesn't matter. I've decided we're selling it. I can't make it work. I just can't."

I grabbed her arm. "Mom! Come on. Don't give up yet. We haven't even opened."

She shook my hand loose. "Please, Isabel. Just stop. My mind is made up."

"I know you're scared, but you'll feel better once we open. I know you will. It's just the unknown right now that's making it hard."

She stood at the sink, staring past me. "Nothing has ever gone my way. Why should this be any different?"

And when she said that, I felt an electrifying current run through my body. I thought of Sophie and how I'd gotten so mad at her. How I'd complained to Grandma about nothing going my way. How I'd pushed Sophie away because I felt like that.

I looked at my mother, standing there, so sad and afraid. And I knew one thing as sure as I knew I'd love New York City. I didn't want to be like my mother.

Chapter 15

cherries jubilee cupcakes

JUST LIKE LOVE, IT'S OH-SO-SWEET

Dad asked me to leave so he could have a private talk with Mom, so I showered and left.

I wasn't sure exactly where I was going, but I had an idea. I just needed to find a little courage first. I ran into Lana downstairs as she walked through the door, carrying a grocery bag. Her hair was tied back in a ponytail and she wore overalls splattered in paint.

"Hey, Isabel, how's it going?"

I sighed and leaned up against the wall. "I don't know. Wait. That's not true. I do know. Terrible."

"Oh, no. Sorry to hear that." She paused, like she was trying to decide if she should say the next thing she was thinking. "Well, do you have a few minutes? I'll show you what I do when I need a pick-me-up."

I shrugged. "Sure."

I followed her upstairs and into her apartment. She put the bag of groceries on the counter. Then she waved at me to follow her toward the back of the apartment.

The second bedroom in her apartment wasn't a bedroom at all. She had turned it into a painting studio, with canvas and easels set up around the room and a big drawing table next to the window.

The paintings were incredible. One of them was a picture of a hillside, with rolling green hills and little flowers blooming in the sun. Another was a picture of the beach with a little girl walking in the sand. It looked so real, it was like I was looking out the window, watching the blond-haired girl walk along the water, admiring the big blue ocean.

Lana went to the closet and grabbed a long white jacket and handed it to me. "I have a friend who is a scientist. Lab coats make great smocks."

I put it on and buttoned it closed in the front while she tore off two big pieces of paper from a roll that sat in the corner.

She laid them in the middle of the floor, and then she went to a bookshelf and picked up some pie tins. Lana took bottles of paint off another shelf and squirted some paint into the tins.

"Okay, Isabel, when was the last time you painted with your fingers?"

I smiled. "Um, never?"

Her mouth opened wide. "What? You've never finger-painted?"

I shook my head.

She smiled back at me. "Well, this will be fun!"

She dropped to her knees, stuck her fingers into the blue, and then swirled it around at the top of her piece of white paper. Then she put her hands in some white and went back and mixed it in with the blue swirls she had just made. The blobs started to look like clouds.

"Cool!" I said.

I kneeled next to her and stuck my fingers in some red. It felt cold, wet and kind of sticky. On the paper, I swirled my fingers around and around, making big and little circles.

I did the same with the blue, and when the blue and red mixed, I had red and blue on the paper, but I also had purple.

"Purplicious," I whispered.

"It's fun to mix colors, isn't it?" Lana said.

I looked at her paper where she had painted clouds and the sun and was working on a flower growing out of the ground. She'd done that all with her fingers!

Mine looked like something a two-year-old would do. Just color and squiggles. And suddenly I wanted more color. More squiggles.

I put all my fingers in the paint this time, then moved them hard across the page, in big, sweeping motions, going this way and that way. Soon there weren't any distinct lines, but instead, waves of color across the page.

Finally I dipped my index finger in the red, and right in the middle of the wavy mess, I painted a heart.

I leaned back and looked at it. Lana stopped what she was doing and looked with me.

"It's beautiful," she said. "What does it make you think of?"

"My insides," I said. "Waves of love, of anger, of sadness, of everything, all mixed together."

She nodded. "But that heart you drew? That shows me that love is the thing that matters most to you. That even when everything is messy, your love is there, shining through."

"Do you think that might be a wave of courage?" I asked, pointing to a brownish-grayish wave of paint next to the heart.

She smiled. "You know, that looks *exactly* like a wave of courage. Wow. How did you draw that so clearly?"

I stood up and grabbed the picture. "Thanks, Lana. That was fun. I think I'm going to take this and give it to someone."

"You might want to let it dry first," she said. "It's pretty wet."

"That's okay. If I walk over, it'll dry on the way."

We went out to the kitchen and washed our hands. I took the smock off and handed it to her.

"Thanks again, Lana," I told her as I walked to the front door. "I hope she likes it."

She wiped her damp hands on the front of her overalls. "Actually, Isabel, I'm pretty sure she'll love it."

I went home to tell Dad I was going to Sophie's, and then I started on the long walk to the yellow duplex. I held the picture flat in my hands, so it could dry in the warm rays of the sun, Lana's words echoing in my ears.

When everything is messy, your love is there, shining through.

I hoped with all my heart Sophie would see that too.

Chapter 16

peach cobbler
cupcakes
PERFECT FOR FAMILY GATHERINGS

J'm pretty sure the walk to Sophie's that warm August day was one of the longest ones of my entire life.

When I got there, Hayden answered the door, talking to me through the screen door, Daisy barking like crazy behind him. "What's the secret password?"

"Huh?" I asked.

"What's the password?"

"Um, open sesame?"

"Bo-ring."

"Okay. How about, Mars is red?"

He raised his eyebrows and smiled. "I like it. You may enter."

I walked through the door, and Daisy jumped on me as if to say, *Notice me, love me, pet me!*

"Alien invasion, alien invasion!" Hayden yelled.

"Hey, who are you calling an alien?" I asked as I bent down to pet the dog. She rolled over, giving me her little white belly to scratch.

If only my life could be as easy as a dog's, I thought.

"Alien or not, Daisy sure is happy to see you." I looked up. Sophie stood there, looking cute as always, wearing black shorts and a frilly yellow blouse.

I stood up, my heart beating quickly in my chest. I swallowed hard. "I hope she's not the only one," I said softly.

"Chickarita," she said. "To my room."

I followed her there. Her room smelled good, like baby powder. She sat on her bed, bouncing up and down slightly. I could tell she was nervous too.

"I'm sorry," I said. "I was a jerk. Jealous of you, I guess." I went over and kneeled in front of her. "I brought you a peace offering. Please, forgive me?"

She laughed and pulled me to my feet. "Stop it. Of course I forgive you. And I'm sorry for criticizing your answer during the interview. I was just trying to help. The last thing I wanted to do was upset you."

I nodded. "I know."

She took the picture from my hands. "Wow, this is cool. Did you make it?"

I wiggled my fingers in front of her face. "With my very own hands."

She laid it on her nightstand. "I love it. Thanks, Is. So, did you see the picture of us? In the paper?"

I rolled my eyes. "Unfortunately."

"It's fine. And the article is good. I predict big sales."

I sat on her bed. "Well, I predict no sales. Mom wants to sell the place. I shouldn't be surprised. I mean, the woman is afraid to get on an airplane. Actually, I'm pretty sure she's afraid to do *anything*."

"You're so not like her," she said.

I looked at her. "What? You don't think so? Sometimes I worry I'm too much like her."

She shook her head. "No way. If I handed you a ticket to Peru right now, you'd go. Even though it's a billion miles away and who knows what kind of food you'd eat there or if they have humongous spiders that kill people. You wouldn't hesitate. You would just go. And that day the reporter came over? Most people would have stayed in their room, using the worst hair day in the history of the universe as their excuse. But not you. You went out there and did what you needed to do."

Daisy nudged the door open with her nose, ran in, and jumped onto the bed in between us. Both of us reached over to pet her.

"But I really didn't do what I needed to do. I didn't help my mom at all. My answer to that reporter's question was so lame. And I knew it. *You* did what needed to be done. *You* knew the right thing to say. Not me. And that's why I got mad. Because I wish I could be more like you."

"What do you mean?"

"You're so determined, Sophie. And you know what you want."

She stood up and faced me. "So tell me. What do *you* want?"

I sighed and put my head in my hands. "I just want to get out of Willow." I looked at her. "Get away from this place that seems to makes my mother crazy. I can't stand it."

She crossed her arms over her chest. "Can't stand what? Willow? Or your mother?"

It felt like she'd stuck a knife in my chest. It hurt. It hurt so much, tears came from deep inside that tender, hurting place in my heart.

As soon as she said it, I knew she was right. It wasn't Willow I wanted to get away from. It was my own mother. Because I had no idea how to relate to her. To talk to her. To help her. All those years I'd tried, I could never understand why she couldn't be happy. Why wasn't being my mom enough? Why was she always looking so hard for something else to make her happy?

Sophie sat down and wrapped her arms around me. She let me cry for a long time.

"I'm sorry," I told her when I pulled away, because my nose was running a lot and I didn't want to get snot on her pretty yellow blouse.

"Me too," she said. "I shouldn't have let you wear that stupid hat. See? I'm not so perfect either."

When I got back to the apartment, I didn't go home. I went into the cupcake shop. It was Sunday, and the workers weren't around. The door was locked, but our apartment key also opened the shop door, so I was able to get in.

The glass cases were all assembled and in place. They looked amazing. I could just picture tray after tray of little cupcakes in various colors and flavors. Next to the cases was a light pink counter. I went and stood behind the newly purchased cash register sitting on the counter.

"Oh, good morning, Mrs. Johnson. What can I get for you? One dozen banana cream pie and one dozen carrot cake? Are you sure on the carrot cake? Oh, of course, yes, they're your husband's favorite. Yes, I know, men can be odd about their food choices, can't they?"

"And what will it be for you, Stan? Oh, why yes, of course, the chocolate coconut are jolly good indeed. Three dozen, you say? Oh, I hope we have enough. It's been busy today."

I could picture it all so clearly, it was as if I'd done it a thousand times. The cupcakes, the people, the fun conversation.

I turned around and ran my finger along the clean counter where just yesterday, Grandma and I had worked, making cupcake after delicious cupcake.

I pulled the passport book out and wrote this:

Food brings people together.
All over the world,
people gather together and eat.
In America, churches have potlucks
and neighborhoods have barbecues.
I like that about America.
—IB

My family needed the cupcake shop. Because we needed to be brought together.

Chapter 17

chocolate caramel cupcakes

THERE'S A HIDDEN TREASURE

INSIDE EACH ONE

Visiting the cupcake shop gave me an idea. A great idea. An incredible idea. An idea that I could only hope Mom would like.

I did what I needed to do to set the idea in motion, and then I went to find Mom. She was sitting next to Dad on the couch, reading a magazine while he watched a baseball game.

I sat down next to her and took a deep breath. "Mom, I want to tell you something."

"Isabel, I don't think—," my dad began.

"Dad, please. Maybe you don't think this is a good idea, but I need to do this. I need Mom to hear me say that I want to bake cupcakes with her. Remember, Mom? We used to bake all the time, and we loved it. That's all this is—another baking session, just a little bigger this time. We're throwing stuff in the bowl, and yeah, it's a big mess for a while. But we'll keep stirring, and we'll cross our fingers, and we'll hope that when we pull the batch out of the oven, it will be something wonderful. A wonderful cupcake shop, just like you wanted."

She didn't say anything. I stood up and took the books that I'd gotten from the library off the coffee table and set them in her lap.

"Mom, we can do this. You believed once, right? Just believe again. If you'll try, meet me in the cupcake shop tomorrow morning at nine. I have a surprise for you."

I walked out and down the hall toward the front door. "Dad, is it all right if I go see Stan and Judy for a few minutes?"

He nodded, so I left.

Stan was home, since it was his day off. And Judy was there too. I'd only talked to her once or twice, but she made me feel like I'd been to their home a hundred times.

"Come in and sit down, Isabel," she said. "I'll get you some lemonade. And we have cookies. You like cookies, right?"

"Yes, thanks."

Their apartment was a lot like ours, although much cooler, since they had an air conditioner. It had old furniture that had seen better days. Bookcases filled with books once read, now just taking up space. And lots of pictures hung on the wall. Stan sat in a big, stuffed green chair. I sat across from him, on the floral couch.

"Nice article in the paper today," he said. "Good

photo, too. I bet you have a ton of business on opening day."

"I hope so," I replied. "Hey, is that your son?" I pointed to one of the pictures on the wall.

"Yes," he said, smiling proudly. "Yes, it is. He lives in Texas now. He should be coming for a visit around Thanksgiving."

"Were you close?" I asked. "When he was growing up?"

Judy brought me a glass of lemonade and a plate with two cookies. "Are you kidding? They fought all the time. They're very different from each other."

I took a bite of the peanut butter cookie. It tasted good. I hadn't had a cookie in so long, it made me want to go home and bake some. "What do you mean?" I asked.

Stan leaned back and put his feet on the stool in front of him. "He loved to be busy doing things. Going places. Seeing things. Me? I like sitting around, talking to people. That's why I like cutting people's hair. All day long I get to hear interesting stories from people."

I nodded and kept eating my cookie.

"Like yesterday, this guy Rupert was telling me how he went to a rummage sale at his church, and he's walking down the aisle, looking at all the junk. And then he spots this long, skinny black case. And he's thinking, what could be in that case? Of course he looked, and it was a sword with this old-looking handle and some papers inside written in what seemed to be Japanese. It looked interesting, so he bought it. Well, he did some checking, and do you know that sword is from the 1800s and is worth thousands of dollars?"

"Really?" I asked. "How much did he pay for it?"

"You won't believe it."

I set the empty plate down on the coffee table. "How much? Like a hundred dollars?"

"Two dollars and fifty cents!" Stan slapped his knee and laughed. "Can you believe that craziness?"

"Is he going to keep it or sell it?" I asked.

"Ahhh, see, you're like me. You want to know more. And to me? That's the most important part of the story. Sure, finding a treasure is exciting, but what are you going to *do* with the treasure?"

"Well?" I asked. "What did he do?"

Stan started laughing again. I liked his laugh. When he laughed, it was like his whole body laughed, not just his mouth. Like he felt the happiness in every bone of his body.

He pulled out a handkerchief and wiped his forehead with it. "Well, he said he's going to keep it. Because just looking at it and thinking about it, like where it's been and how it's survived this long, is an amazing thing. He said he can always sell it if he needs the money someday. But for now, the treasure makes him happy."

I nodded as I thought about that. Owning the sword made him feel good. And that was enough.

"Stan!" I said, jumping up. "That's it! We need to get my mom to understand that it's not about the money or success or any of that. It's about the *treasure*. It's about having a cupcake shop and sharing with the people who visit every day. Who cares if Beatrice's Brownies sells more than we do? It doesn't really matter, does it?"

He smiled. "I think you're right, Isabel. I may not be living in a mansion, and I'm sure there are plenty more successful barber shops than mine. But who cares? Mine is perfect for me."

"Can I borrow your phone? That's why I came here, actually. I need to call my grandma, to tell her to meet me downstairs in the morning. I didn't want my parents to hear, because it's a surprise."

He pointed toward the kitchen. "Help yourself. Have another cookie if you'd like too."

As I walked toward the kitchen, he said, "Knock-knock."

"Who's there?"

"Sherwood."

"Sherwood who?"

"Sherwood like to have a cupcake shop down-stairs!"

"Me too," I told Stan. "Me too."

I talked to Grandma, and she agreed to come over at nine o'clock, bringing something with her that I needed. I asked Stan to be there too and to bring a little something as well.

When I left and went back home, I knew I had done everything I could.

Now it was up to Mom.

I bet it's scary sometimes,
traveling in a new place.
But you take along maps
and a cell phone,
and you know help is there
if you need it.
—IB

Chapter 18

grandma's applesauce cupcakes

TASTE JUST LIKE HOME

The next morning I woke up early. Like six a.m. early. I got dressed, then grabbed my keys and the envelope of babysitting money I'd been saving. I reached inside the envelope and pulled out the small pile of bills, fanning it the way I'd seen thieves do it on TV. Except I wasn't a thief. I'd worked hard for that money, hoping to see something besides the sidewalks of Willow, Oregon. I felt a little twinge of pain about giving it up, but a little voice inside me told me I would travel someday. Just not today.

Besides, I'd been thinking it was just like Stan said. Maybe it wasn't really going places and seeing things that mattered. Maybe it was just doing your best to enjoy the people around you. Like that day with Lucas and Logan. While the pool filled with water, I should have taken my shoes off and gotten in the pool with them. I should have splashed and laughed and stopped thinking about those books and what I *didn't* have, and instead just been glad for what I *did* have.

I tiptoed out the front door and down the stairs and went around to the front door of the cupcake shop.

What I saw when I walked inside the shop made me smile so big, my cheeks felt like they were going to crack to pieces.

All night long Lana had stayed up, painting a mural on one of the walls to look like a rolling countryside with green hills, a big tree in the corner, and a bright blue sky. No matter how rainy it might be outside, people would feel like they were sitting next to a sunny countryside inside our little shop. It was perfect.

"Lana," I squealed. "It's so beautiful."

She wiped her hands on her overalls and carefully walked down the ladder. "The tree isn't finished yet." She looked at her watch. "I should have it done by nine, though."

I couldn't stop looking at it. "Beatrice's Brownies might have Dixie cups full of milk, but they have *nothing* like this." I turned and looked at her. "You must be so tired. Thank you. Thank you very much."

"You're welcome, Isabel. I hope your mom likes it. I hope it makes her excited to be in the cupcake business."

I handed Lana the envelope of money. "I know you probably get paid a lot more than this. But it's all I have."

"No worries," she said, taking the envelope. "I'm happy to help you guys out. And you can pay me the rest in cupcakes, how's that?"

I reached out my hand. "Deal."

I sat and watched Lana paint for a while. But I

didn't want to make her nervous, so I went back upstairs and put on the coffee. While it dripped into the pot, I wrote in my passport book:

> *People travel to see beautiful things.*
> *But really, beauty is everywhere,*
> *isn't it?*
> *—IB*

Dad came out, and I'm pretty sure I was still smiling like a chimpanzee, because he asked me, "What are you up to, young lady?"

"You'll see," I said. "Do you think she's going to show up?"

He went in the kitchen and pulled a mug out of the cupboard. "I don't know, honey. I hope so."

I went downstairs to wait. Lana was cleaning up, so I helped her carry the paint back upstairs to her apartment. It was good to have something to keep me busy.

At 8:50 Grandma showed up with the pink ribbon and the thumbtacks like I had asked her to. She was dressed in pink from head to toe for the occasion.

Literally. Pink suit, pink hat, and pink shoes.

When she walked in and saw the mural, her hand flew to her mouth as she let out a big gasp. "Oh, Izzy, it's incredible."

"I know," I said, stepping back to admire it again with her. "Lana, our neighbor, did it for us. Do you think Mom will like it?"

She came and gave me a hug. "She's going to love it. That was so sweet of you."

We strung the pretty ribbon from one end of the store to the other, straight across, about waist high.

I looked at my watch. Nine o'clock.

"You want me to go check on her?" Grandma asked.

I shook my head. "She has to do it on her own."

9:05. 9:10.

Grandma paced the floor, her heels clicking on the parquet floor as she walked.

I heard the door open and quickly turned around.

"Hey, sorry we're late," Stan said, with Judy next to him. "Is she here yet?"

I shook my head. "Not yet." My shoulders slumped. "Maybe she's not coming. Why should today be different from any other day? I'm so stupid. Just because I go in there, hand her some books, and tell her I have a surprise for her, I think that's going to make a difference?"

Grandma came over and put her arm around me. "Why should today be any different? Because, my dear Izzy, you just never know. Maybe reaching out to her yesterday, in the special way that only you can, is just what she needed. Why, I remember one time, I was feeling down about the state of the economy and worried about your grandfather's business in the worst way. And about that time, I got the nicest letter from Patricia Nixon. You know, President Nixon's wife? I had written her a letter because I wanted her to know I was thinking about her while her husband was going through a terrible time. Well, she wrote me back, and that letter did wonders for my spirits. It was a simple gesture. But it meant so much."

I heard a noise and looked up. The door opened slowly, Mom's face visible through the glass at the top of the door. I held my breath, waiting for her to see the wall behind me.

Dad came in right after her. When she walked in, she looked at me, and then I watched as she noticed the rolling hills and the blue sky. I moved to the side so she could take it all in. Just like Grandma, her hand flew to her mouth in shock. Then her eyes got crinkly and tears started to form.

I ran to her and gently grabbed her elbow. "Mom, don't cry. Don't you like it?"

"Oh, Isabel, I think it's just about the most beautiful thing I've ever seen. You did this for me?"

I looked around the room. "Well, I think I did it for all of us."

She nodded and turned to give me a hug. "I'm so sorry," she whispered. "I'm working on an attitude adjustment, I promise."

When she pulled away, she looked around the room. "Thanks for being here, everyone."

Stan walked toward Mom with a pair of scissors in his hand. "Caroline, these have been very lucky for me over the years. Not once have I cut off an ear or scratched a cheek." We laughed. "Will you please do the honors and cut your ribbon? This shop is your little treasure. Cherish it. Share it. Love it. And I promise, when you do that, others will love it too."

"Thanks, Stan," she said as she took the scissors from his hand. She looked over at me. "And thank you, Isabel. Thanks for continuing to stir to make something wonderful when I couldn't do it. You're the best."

She looked around the room one last time. And then, without any hesitation, she cut the ribbon.

And we all clapped for a really, really long time.

Chapter 19

lucky lemon-lime cupcakes

BETTER THAN A FOUR-LEAF CLOVER

To say we were busy the first couple of weeks doesn't even begin to describe it. We were slammed. But of course, it was all good, and Mom's confidence grew, thank goodness.

A storm blew through, and it rained the first few days we were open, which meant that all the moms who would normally take their kids to play in the fountain in the park brought them to our place to have cupcakes instead. Mom said it was entirely appropriate that it rained on the day It's Raining Cupcakes opened.

Everyone we knew, plus many more we didn't, showed up the first day. I couldn't believe how many teachers from the middle school came. I think Mr. Nelson must have sent them all a note or something. He stopped by too and brought some cool pictures of Washington, D.C., with him.

Sue Canova brought her twin boys by for a cupcake, and when she saw me, she gave me a hug and told me there were no hard feelings. At least I think that's what she said. The boys were jumping up and down and yelling, "Cupcakes, cupcakes, CUPCAKES!" so it was a little hard to hear.

But the best surprise was having Aunt Christy drop by. She came right from the airport, still dressed in her flight attendant uniform. She gave me a bag of goodies from different places she'd visited in the past couple of months. My favorite souvenir was a miniature Statue of Liberty. I'd been checking the mail every day, expecting to hear about the baking contest, one way or the other. But so far I hadn't heard a thing.

Christy couldn't stay long, as she had another flight that evening, to Chicago. We sent her on her way with a belly full of cupcakes, which she said was icing on the cupcake after visiting with us for a while.

As she left, she told us she would tell all the people traveling to Oregon to make sure they stopped in at It's Raining Cupcakes. I know Mom appreciated that a lot.

The first day, we opened at noon and ran out of cupcakes by three. People were really nice, though, and sat at the little pink tables drinking coffee or tea and talking about how they'd just have to come back the next day and get some cupcakes.

The next morning Grandma, Mom, and I tripled the number of cupcakes we made. This time, we had enough to get us through our regular closing time, five o'clock.

Mom had decided that for all our sakes, the shop would be open five days a week, Tuesday through Saturday, and only in the afternoons. "We don't want to work ourselves to death," she'd said.

Beatrice's Brownies had a great opening weekend, of course. We got in line with everyone else to check it out. The brownies were good, but their chocolaty goodness didn't make any of us cry in despair or anything. By then Mom knew her cupcake shop was special in and of itself.

The day after Labor Day, Dad and I had to go back to school. Grandma and Mom said they'd be fine without us and not to worry. Still, I did—just a little.

Sophie and I ended up with three classes together, which made us extremely happy. She came home with me after school, so we could talk about our first day.

"I miss Kyle so much," she said, as we sat at the kitchen table, drinking some iced tea before we went downstairs to see how Mom and Grandma were doing.

"Has he written you back yet?" I asked.

She shook her head. "I can't believe it. I thought we had something special, you know? But that reminds me. Guess what I did get in the mail?"

"What?"

"A letter telling me I didn't place in the baking contest. I'm so bummed. Did you get one?"

I shook my head. "Maybe I should run down and check the mail right now." I started to get up and find the mail key when the phone rang. I thought it might be Mom calling from downstairs to ask why we hadn't come to see her yet.

"Hello?" I said.

"May I speak to Isabel Browning?" a woman on the other end said.

"This is she."

"Isabel, this is Julia from *Baker's Best* magazine. I'm so glad you answered the phone. I'm calling to let you know that you are one of our finalists for the baking contest you entered last month. Congratulations!"

I backed up against the counter and grabbed onto it to keep myself steady. "Are you serious?"

She chuckled. "I'm very serious. We loved your recipe. It was so different from anything else submitted. Very original."

Sophie came over with a puzzled look on her face. *Who is it?* she mouthed.

I covered the mouthpiece with my hand and whispered, "The baking contest."

"Isabel, is everything all right?" Julia asked.

"Yes, sorry. I just can't believe I'm really a finalist!"

By now Sophie was clapping her hands together really fast, although quietly, and jumping up and down.

"Isabel, we look forward to seeing you in New York in November. You'll get a packet in the mail in the next week with all the information. Please give it to your parent or guardian who will be accompanying you on the trip, so it can be completed and mailed back to us right away."

"Okay, I will. Thank you very much."

"Congratulations again, Isabel. Bye."

When I hung up, Sophie grabbed my hands and pulled me around in circles. "You get to go to New York, you get to go to New York!"

I laughed as we spun around and around. When we stopped, we stood there, holding hands. I squeezed hers and said, "I'm so sorry, Soph. You didn't place."

She reached out and hugged me. "It's okay! You get to go on a trip, just like you wanted. That's more than enough to make me happy."

"Thanks, Soph."

"Come on. We have to tell your mom and your grandma. They are going to die when they hear!"

I gulped. "That's what I'm afraid of." But she pulled me along, smiling like there wasn't a thing to worry about.

As we walked downstairs, I said, "Sophie, what did you want the thousand dollars for, anyway? You never really told me."

She stopped before we went through the door and closed one eye, like she was thinking. "I'm not sure I want to tell you."

I put my hands on my hips. "What? What do you mean? Come on. You have to tell me."

"Okay, fine. But you can't tell anyone. Promise?"

"Promise."

"I want to take acting lessons. And singing lessons too." She smiled. "You know how much I loved those theater camps. My mom found some more for next year that I can do with other teens. But when she talked to the camp director, he said a lot of the kids take professional lessons throughout the year. And if I want to get better, so I can be a professional actress someday—"

"Oh, Sophie Bird," I said, "you will make a *maahvelous* actress someday. I can just see you on the big screen. When you move to Hollywood, can I come and visit?"

She laughed. "Absolutely, Chickarita. Just be prepared. I don't think it's anything like Willow."

We kept giggling and talking as we made our way to the cupcake shop. Lana was sitting at a table with a cup of tea, reading a book. I waved at her, and she waved back. The other tables were filled with people I didn't recognize. That was a good sign. It meant people were coming because they'd heard the cupcakes were good, not because they knew us.

We walked back into the kitchen. It smelled yummy, like always. A mix of cinnamon, vanilla, and chocolate all rolled into one. Grandma greeted me with a hug. Mom had bought each of them official cupcake "uniforms" to force Grandma to stop wearing fancy dresses to work. I almost hadn't recognized her the first day she showed up in khaki pants and a pink T-shirt with the words IT'S RAINING CUPCAKES printed on the front.

She'd said, "Now I'll have to style my hair every day. That's the real reason I wear hats, you know. Nothing like a hat to fix a bad hair day." It made me laugh, because I knew about that trick!

When I saw Mom, my insides felt like someone had taken a mixer to them. She walked over and put her hand on my forehead. "You don't look very good, Isabel. Is everything all right?"

"Mom," I said, my voice shaking just a little, "remember that baking contest?"

"Of course I remember."

"Well, they called to say that I'm one of the finalists."

She squealed and clapped her hands together. "Isabel, that's wonderful!"

I gulped. "You know the bake-off is in New York, right? An adult has to go with me. Do you think Dad can get some time off work in November to take me?"

Mom walked over to the counter and opened a drawer. She pulled out a book and held it up. It was

"I liked it so much, I bought my own copy," she said. "I've been doing visualization exercises. If I keep at it, I bet I'll be ready to go in November." Mom turned to my grandma. "You can keep things running for a few days, can't you, Mom?"

"Of course," she said. "I'll be happy to."

I couldn't believe it. I let out a big sigh of relief. She was really going to try. Try to get over her fears. For me.

Mom looked at me. "Oh, I can't wait to visit St. Valentine's Cupcakes! And take you to a Broadway play. And—"

Sophie grabbed our hands and started jumping up and down. "You're going to New York, you're going to New York!"

As I giggled at silly Sophie, I noticed something out of the corner of my eye. I turned and looked, which made everyone look. A young guy with a mustache and major bedhead hair stood there, holding a laundry basket full of clothes.

"Can I help you?" Mom asked.

"I think I'm lost," he said. "I'm looking for the Bleachorama."

Mom turned around and looked at me, and I could tell she was trying not to laugh. We were both thinking of that day I had asked her where the people would go who needed to wash their clothes.

She walked around to the front and took his basket from him. "Mother, will you get him a cupcake and some milk, please? I'm going to take these upstairs and wash them for him."

"Wow," he said. "That's some service. A place that does laundry and gives you cupcakes. I'll have to tell all my friends."

"NO!" we all shouted. Then we burst out laughing.

But as Mom walked out the door, she turned around with a twinkle in her eye. "You know, now that I think about it, you could be onto something there. I mean, Beatrice's Brownies certainly doesn't—"

"You have an adorable cupcake shop, just like you wanted," I said, interrupting her, as I walked over and put my arm around her. "Let's leave it at that, okay, Mom?"

She looked around and smiled a relaxed, happy smile. "I do, don't I?"

Later that night, I wrote in my passport booklet as I daydreamed about our trip to New York City.

I journeyed to a place
where it's always raining cupcakes.
I didn't need a passport,
but I met a lot of interesting people
and experienced new things.
Even though the trip was a little bumpy,
I got there just fine.
—IB

Chapter 20

the dr. seuss cupcake

THIS ONE WILL SURPRISE YOU!

When we arrived at our hotel, I called Dad and then Grandma to let them know the flight went just fine. Mom brought along a special compact disc Aunt Christy had sent her for people afraid of flying. She played it during both the takeoff and the landing to help her relax. It seemed to work. The rest of the time, she browsed cooking magazines, looking for inspiration for new cupcake flavors.

As for me, I felt nervous and excited and a hundred other things, so I didn't know what to do with myself. Mostly I just looked out the window and tried to enjoy every minute of the flight. I loved it when we took off—it didn't scare me at all. As we flew higher and higher, I watched the buildings and roads get smaller and smaller. Eventually, it looked like a town for dolls—everything was so tiny. But my favorite part was approaching New York and seeing the Statue of Liberty from the plane. I got all teary-eyed, and when I looked at Mom, she was right there with me. Incredible.

The cab ride to our hotel was a different story. I swear I almost peed my pants! There were cars everywhere, and lots of honking going on. Our driver didn't speak English very well, so we couldn't understand much of anything he said, even though he talked to us almost the entire time. I wanted to tell him to be quiet and just drive. I kept grabbing Mom's leg when he'd slam on his brakes or squeeze in between two cars in another lane. I should have asked Mom for her relaxation CD.

Finally we made it to our hotel in one piece. Mom and I were superexcited, because the magazine had put us in a hotel right in the middle of Times Square.

"Do you think we'll see anyone famous?" I asked her.

"That would be fun, wouldn't it? But just think, Isabel, after you win that baking contest, *you'll* be the one who's famous!"

Every time she mentioned the contest, my stomach felt like I was on another cab ride. I told myself I didn't care if I won or not. It didn't really matter, because I'd gotten to take a great trip, and that was the best prize of all. Still, part of me did want to win, because it'd be something I'd remember forever. And also because I knew Mom hoped to get some free publicity out of the deal.

We had Friday afternoon and evening to do whatever we wanted, and then early Saturday morning a car would pick us up and drive us to the bake-off. Saturday night we would attend a fancy banquet, where the grand prize would be awarded to the winner. Then Sunday we'd be on our own again, to do more sightseeing before we flew back home Monday morning.

After we got settled into our hotel room, which was small but nice, we headed right out to our first stop—St. Valentine's Cupcakes. Out of all the things we planned on seeing and doing, I think the cupcake shop made Mom the most excited.

We got directions from a man at the front desk, then we went outside and started walking. Just like I imagined, the street felt like one big beehive, buzzing with people. Almost everyone walked fast, so Mom and I found ourselves hurrying too, even though we had no reason to. I could just imagine Sophie there, making fun of the way everyone walked, and then going slow on purpose just to be different and annoy people.

The cupcake shop looked like something from a TV show. I knew it would be beautiful—but *wow*. First of all, the place was huge, like five times the size of our little shop. Round tables were surrounded by lovely chairs with deep red seat cushions and high chair backs made of brass with a heart shape at the top of each one. The walls were painted a shiny gold color, and different heart-shaped paintings hung on them. The glass cases that displayed the cupcakes went from one end of the room to the other end and wrapped around in a big L shape. I couldn't believe how many cupcakes there were to choose from!

The line went all the way out the door, and shortly after we arrived, it made its way down the sidewalk.

"See," I told Mom, "people get just as excited about cupcakes as they do about brownies."

She smiled as she looked at a menu she had picked up from a stand by the door. "What kind are you going to get?"

I shrugged. "I don't know. How do you even choose?"

"I'm going to get the Lucky Lemon-Lime. Figure we can use all the luck we can get for tomorrow."

The lady behind us leaned in and smiled. She was about Mom's age, with warm brown eyes. She wore a red knitted hat with a cute little bow just above the brim. "I'm getting a dozen of those for a party tonight, along with a dozen of the Dr. Seuss. They're all wonderful, but those two flavors are my favorite."

"There's a cupcake called the Dr. Seuss?" I asked. "What's it made out of? Green eggs and ham?"

That made her laugh. "I don't really know. They keep it a secret. But trust me, it's fabulous!"

When we reached the counter, I decided to try the Dr. Seuss. We also ordered some tea, which came in the most adorable little teapot I'd ever seen, in the shape of a white rabbit.

We took a seat, and Mom bit into her cupcake. "Mmmm, Isabel, it's magnificent. Try yours."

I started to peel the paper off. "Maybe we should have come here after the bake-off. My s'mores cupcakes are going to seem so ordinary now."

Mom stopped chewing, and her eyes got big and round. "Isabel. Don't you know? Didn't she tell you on the phone?"

"Know what? What do you mean?"

"Honey, you aren't baking cupcakes tomorrow. You're baking chocolate tarts."

I blinked my eyes. I blinked them again. Did I hear her right? No, I couldn't have.

"What?" I asked. "What are you talking about?"

She smiled. "I saw that tart recipe sitting on the counter. And the jam tarts in the garbage can. They looked incredible. So I made a batch myself, in the shop's kitchen one day. Isabel, they were truly out of this world. I ran out and got a copy of the magazine, found the address, and mailed the tart recipe for you, just in time to meet the deadline."

"But, but—" It was hard to find the words as my brain tried to understand what she was saying. "You mean I submitted two recipes? Is that even legal?"

"The entry form said you could enter up to three."

"But how do we know the tart recipe won?" I asked.

She reached into her purse and pulled out the papers I had given her to complete. "It says right here, in the letter they sent with the paperwork."

I followed her finger and read the very last line of the letter. "We are looking forward to meeting you as well as Isabel, and tasting her delicious chocolate jam tarts!"

"I'm sorry, sweetie," she said. "I was wrong to make you feel like you had to enter a cupcake recipe. I get so wrapped up in my own stuff sometimes, I forget what's really important."

I didn't have time to say anything. The lady with the red hat came by our table, carrying her boxes of cupcakes. "What do you think?" She looked at my cupcake with no bites taken out of it. "What? You haven't tried it yet? Well, go on, try it!"

I reached down and took a bite. First I tasted chocolate. Then I tasted something sweet and crunchy. Jelly beans! But there was something else I couldn't quite figure out.

I sat there chewing and thinking. "I know. Bananas! Chocolate, jelly beans, and bananas. It's so good! It's like they threw a bunch of stuff into a bowl, not sure how it would turn out, and surprise, it turned out fantastic!"

My mom looked at me, and then up at the lady, and said, "I need to remember that cupcake when I'm worrying about whether or not things are going to turn out okay."

She laughed and said, "You and me both. Where are you ladies from, anyway?"

"Willow, Oregon," Mom said as she reached into her purse and grabbed a business card. "I own a cupcake shop there, as a matter of fact."

The lady took her card. "Wow, you've come a long way, haven't you? Well, enjoy your trip!" She waved and disappeared into the hive of buzzing New Yorkers with her boxes of scrumptious cupcakes.

"You know, Isabel," Mom said as I took another bite of my cupcake, "I brought along one of my It's Raining Cupcakes T-shirts. I was going to wear it tomorrow, but maybe it'd get more attention if you wore it. What do you think?"

I smiled. "Sure. I can do that."

When we got back to the hotel, I bought postcards in the gift shop.

Dear Dad,

Here's a list of things New York has taught me:

1. Have a tissue ready when you see the Statue of Liberty for the first time.

2. Go to the bathroom before you get into a cab in New York City.

3. Cupcakes can be like people. Sometimes a little different, but still good.

Love, Isabel

S'mores Cupcakes

Cupcakes

1 cup all-purpose flour

¾ cup granulated sugar

½ teaspoon baking soda

½ cup butter or margarine

1/3 cup water

3 tablespoons unsweetened cocoa

1 egg, lightly whisked

¼ cup buttermilk

Frosting

¼ cup unsalted butter, softened

1 ½ cups powdered sugar

½ teaspoon vanilla

1 7-oz. jar marshmallow cream

4 graham cracker squares

15 Hershey Kisses

Preheat oven to 350°. Line muffin tins with cupcake papers.

In a large mixing bowl, mix flour, sugar, and baking soda together with a whisk. In a saucepan, melt the butter/margarine with the water and cocoa on low heat. When completely melted, remove from heat. Whisk egg in a separate bowl and add to flour mixture, along with the melted butter/margarine mixture, buttermilk and vanilla. Beat with electric mixer on low until smooth.

Fill cupcake liners half full. Bake 18–20 minutes, until toothpick inserted into center comes out clean. Let cupcakes cool completely before frosting.

For frosting, beat softened butter, powdered sugar, and vanilla until smooth. Add marshmallow cream and mix. Spread on cooled cupcakes with knife.

Use a food chopper to finely chop graham crackers, or break into pieces and put in a plastic bag and roll over them with a rolling pin. Set aside.

Unwrap candy kisses and place one on top of each cupcake, then sprinkle graham cracker crumbs across the top.

Makes about 15 cupcakes.

Grandma's Applesauce Cupcakes

Cupcakes

3 medium or 2 large Granny Smith apples

½ cup water

cinnamon and sugar mixture

1 1/3 cups all-purpose flour

1 teaspoon baking soda

1 teaspoon baking powder

1 teaspoon ground cinnamon

½ teaspoon nutmeg

¼ teaspoon ground cloves

½ teaspoon salt

½ cup granulated sugar

½ cup firmly packed brown sugar

½ cup canola oil

2 eggs

Frosting

1 8-oz. package cream cheese, softened

½ cup unsalted butter, softened

2 teaspoons vanilla

2 cups powdered sugar

Preheat oven to 350°. Line muffin tins with cupcake papers.

Peel, core, and cut apples into small, bite-size pieces. Place in a large, microwave-safe bowl. Add water and generously sprinkle with cinnamon and sugar. Microwave on high 3 minutes, check and stir, and repeat 3 to 4 times, or until apples have softened to a chunky applesauce texture.

In a small mixing bowl, stir together flour, soda, powder, spices, and salt and set aside. In the mixing bowl with the applesauce, add sugars and oil and whisk together. Whisk eggs in separate bowl. Add to apple mixture and whisk together. Add the flour mixture to the apple mixture slowly, stirring with a wooden spoon until just combined.

Fill the muffin tins about three-quarters full. Bake 20–22 minutes, until toothpick inserted into the center comes out clean. Let cupcakes cool completely before frosting.

For frosting, beat cream cheese and softened butter together with a mixer until smooth. Mix in vanilla. Add powdered sugar and mix until creamy. If you have a pastry bag, you can pipe frosting onto the cupcakes.

Makes about 18 cupcakes. These are best eaten the day they are made.